PTS. 8

RL - 4.9

Cabin
102

Sherry Garland

Cabin 102

Harcourt Brace and Company

San Diego   New York   London

Requests for permission to make copies of any part of
the work should be mailed to: Permissions Department,
Harcourt Brace & Company, 6277 Sea Harbor Drive,
Orlando, Florida 32887-6777.

Library of Congress Cataloging-in-Publication Data
Garland, Sherry.
Cabin 102/Sherry Garland.
p. cm.
Summary: While on a cruise with his family, twelve-
year-old Dusty encounters the ghost of an Arawak Indian
girl, through whom he comes to terms with his fears.
ISBN 0-15-200663-X   ISBN 0-15-200662-1 (pbk.)
[1. Fear—Fiction. 2. Ghosts—Fiction. 3. Ocean
liners—Fiction. 4. Arawak Indians—Fiction. 5. Indians of the West Indies—Fiction.] I. Title.
PZ7.G18414Cab 1995
[Fic]—dc20   95-13414

The text was set in Sabon.
Designed by Lydia D'moch
First edition
A B C D E
A B C D E (pbk.)
Printed in the United States of America

To Donna,
still cruising after all these years

Contents

vii

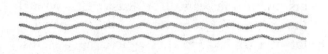

The Big Secret

I'M STANDING ON the jetty watching the ships parade by, their masts and sails black against the setting sun. The water is sloshing against my sneakers as the waves roll in and wash out. There's a hotel across the boulevard and in the hotel is a swimming pool. That's where I lost my friend Bobby. He didn't drown or move away or anything like that. All he did was invite me to his twelfth birthday party.

It was a bright June day and I was spending the summer with my dad on Galveston Island like I had done for the past four years, since the divorce. Bobby and I rode our bikes down the narrow two-lane highway toward Seawall Boulevard, the main drag. We were going to mess around, and check out babes in skimpy bikinis on the seawall. At least that's what I thought until Bobby turned into the parking lot of Paradise Hotel. I figured he was just stopping to catch his breath. Bobby was a plump sort of guy and sometimes couldn't keep up with me.

"Dusty," he said as he straddled his bike and breathed short little gasps. "I've decided I'm going to have that birthday party after all."

"Hey, that's cool," I said. "Wish I coulda had one when I turned twelve last February. Is the party going to be at your house?"

Bobby shook his head and gulped down a big swig of lime Gatorade from the plastic bottle he carried strapped to his bike.

"You won't believe this," he said. "I had this brainstorm a few days ago. Hit me right out of the blue. You see, my uncle is the manager of Paradise Hotel."

"This hotel?" I glanced up at the giant neon palm trees. At night they flashed off and on in shades of bright pink and green and yellow.

Bobby was so excited now that he was waving his hands. "My uncle says that sometimes clients reserve the swimming pool for private parties. And the hotel kitchen is right there to bake a cake and serve up ice cream."

"A swimming party?"

"Yeah, ain't this boy a genius?" He puffed his chest out and patted his own shoulder. "My uncle says he can serve the food right out by the pool. I'm thinking pizza."

A very uneasy feeling began creeping over me. I gripped the handlebars to keep my fingers from shaking.

"Why a swimming party, Bobby? People swim in the ocean every day."

"For the babes, of course," he said with a laugh. "I'm going to invite a bunch of them." He pushed his bike up to a pole and locked the chain. "Come on, let's go around to the swimming pool and check it out. I can't wait. I've already talked to some kids and they all think it's cool."

Bobby kept rattling off details as we walked, but I didn't hear what he was saying. The minute the words "swimming pool" left his lips, my heart had started leaping around in my chest like a herd of frogs. I felt the blood draining from my face, and suddenly the hotel lobby was too hot and there was no air. I stopped at a drinking fountain and shoved my face into the cool water. When I wiped the beads from my lips, I felt my fingers shaking.

We cut through the lobby and entered the

pool area through a black wrought-iron gate surrounded by lush palms, pink oleander bushes, and giant philodendrons. The pool was small, but it had big boulders clustered at the shallow end, and a small waterfall tumbled over them.

Bobby walked right up and stuck his hand in the waterfall. I hung back among the lounge chairs, gripping the handrail along the stone walkway that led to the lobby. But even holding on to it didn't stop the shaking.

All the time Bobby was bragging about his brainchild, I was staring at the swimming pool like a little kid stares at a closet late at night, convinced a gorilla lives in it. I knew exactly what would happen to me if I got in the water. First it would feel like something had grabbed my feet and pulled me down. Then fear like you can't imagine would grip my body. My legs would freeze up and my lungs would cease to work right. Coughing and wheezing, I would barely be able to stagger out of the pool. I might even throw up. And everyone would snicker and laugh or, worse yet, feel pity for me.

The thought of it made my knees turn to jelly, so I plopped down in a deck chair and closed my eyes.

"Dusty? You okay?"

I opened my eyes and saw Bobby standing over me.

"Yeah, must have been something I ate this morning."

"You haven't said anything about my birthday party."

I swallowed hard and my brain began groping for excuses. When it came to getting out of swimming, I was the king of excuses. I had a list a mile long tucked away for every occasion.

"Bobby, my friend," I said as I stood up and put my hands on his shoulders. "You know you're my good friend, but I've got some bad news about this swimming pool."

"What?" Bobby stepped back and crossed his arms.

"Didn't you hear? The police dragged a dead body out of it last week."

"Get outa here! You're crazy. My uncle would have told me about that."

I shrugged. "Sorry, but it gets even more gross than that. I swear this is the pool that some little kids are always pooping and peeing in. They live in one of those condos over there and sneak in at night. I saw a bunch of them in here once after midnight."

Bobby's face turned red and his jaw moved as he gritted his teeth.

"That ain't funny, Dusty. Stop joking around. If you don't want to go to my birthday party, just come out and say so."

"I love birthday parties. You know that. Why don't you have it at your house? We could play baseball in that empty lot next door."

"No way. Mom says no parties at the house. Remember, she just had it remodeled. Besides, you're forgetting the babes in their bikinis." He rubbed his plump hands together like a chipmunk getting ready to devour an acorn.

I ran my fingers through my dark hair. Bobby's heart was set on a pool party. But I couldn't get in the water in front of all those people, especially the girls. I knew how pool parties were. Guys always throwing each other into the water and horsing around. If anyone saw me flailing my arms and screaming, I would become the laughingstock of the island.

"Well?" Bobby demanded.

I took a deep breath and pulled out another excuse.

"Look, Bobby, your birthday is next Saturday, right?"

"Yeah."

"Well, I didn't want to tell you this. It's sort of a secret. But I have a big date with a really cool babe."

"Yeah?" Bobby's sandy-colored eyebrows shot up. He jabbed me in the ribs and grinned. "Hey, why didn't you just say so, man? Who is she?"

Bobby knew who I liked. Heck, every guy on the island my age liked her, too. She was so fine, so popular. And that was my big mistake.

"Jennifer Beauchamp, of course. Who else?"

Bobby's round blue eyes flew open and his jaw dropped. Color flashed across his cheeks. I swear, steam was hissing out of his ears.

"That's it!" he screamed. "You're lying again!"

"What? You don't think I could get a date with Jennifer?"

"Not next Saturday, you can't. She's coming to my birthday party. She already asked her mom and everything."

"Oh." I tried to smile and shrug it off, but Bobby was not amused.

"Why do you lie so much, Dusty? I thought you were my friend."

"I am. I swear."

"No, you're not. Friends don't lie to each

other the way you do." Bobby started walking toward the iron gate. I trotted after him and grabbed his tee shirt by the sleeve.

"Uh, maybe I got my days mixed up. Yeah, that's probably it . . ."

"Forget it, man!" Bobby shrieked. "You're not my friend anymore. And don't worry about making up any more lies; you're not even invited now." He jerked his arm free and stomped through the hotel lobby to where his bicycle was chained up.

I felt my heart drop down around my feet as I watched Bobby ride off like greased lightning. He was the only friend I had left on the island. All the others had gotten sick of my excuses a long time ago, not only here but back in the city where I lived with Mom the rest of the year.

Most of the time my excuses worked. Like this one: Sorry, Mom won't let me go swimming today, I've got a terrible cold *(cough, cough)*. Or this one: What! Go swimming in that pond? You're crazy, man. I just saw a six-foot water moccasin slide down the bank. Or this one: I'd love to go swimming in that lake, but I've heard it's full of mercury poison. You want your hair to fall out, man? Or this old favorite: Hey, you can stay out there in the ocean if you want, but I just saw Jennifer Beau-champ go by in a red bikini. This I've gotta see.

But sometimes those excuses got very com-plicated and backfired, like today. I lost a lot of friends that way. Bobby had been about the last guy I knew who would still talk to me.

I slowly pedaled down the highway back toward my dad's beach house. I guess I should have told Bobby about my fear of water. But it's not easy living during the summer on an island where sand and surf and swimming are everyone's main passion. Even my own mother and father didn't know about my fears.

It was my BIG SECRET, and it had been my secret since I was five years old. That was when I fell into a swimming pool and drowned. I was brought back to life by a big, tanned lifeguard named Lloyd. The only thing I remember about that day was the feeling that something had grabbed me and pulled me un-der. Something with icy hands had wanted me for its plaything. I had slipped out of its clutches that day, jerked free by Lloyd's long, hairy arms and brought back to life by his Listerine-flavored breath.

I was one lucky little kid that day, I guess, but I never could shake the feeling that some-thing down in the water was mad as heck that

I had gotten away. And I knew that I wouldn't be so lucky the next time it got me in its cold, blue fingers. Whenever I got near a river or a lake or especially the ocean, I had the feeling that if I ever fell into deep water I would sink to the bottom and drift away forever in an endless blue pit. Heck, I didn't even like to take baths. That's how I got my nickname, Dusty.

When I finally arrived at the beach house that day, the first thing I saw was my dad in the driveway working on his sailboat. He loved the water—deep-sea fishing, sailing, and especially swimming. He could have been an Olympic swimmer, except that he busted up his knee in a football game one weekend and ruined his chances of glory.

Dad paused with the repairs and pushed his dark-rimmed glasses back up his nose.

"I'm taking the womenfolk sailing after lunch," he called down to me. "Want to come along?"

The thought of being on a tiny sailboat in the middle of the Gulf of Mexico made me shiver.

"No thanks," I said. "I've got to go to the library. I have a bunch of books due back today." That was one of my favorite excuses. Parents hate to tell their kids not to read.

A wave of disappointment, or maybe it was disgust, moved over Dad's face. He glanced at the beach where my new stepmom, Vanessa, and her two daughters, Jasmine and Jessica, were swimming and playing in the surf. The blond bunch I always called them. They must have been half fish, they loved the water so much. Jessica, the oldest one, was on the junior high swim team.

"Okay, suit yourself," Dad said and turned back to his repairs.

I bet he was thanking his lucky stars that he finally had some children who loved swimming as much as he did. Maybe I should have told him about my phobia a long time ago, but how could I? It would break his heart to know that his son was a sniveling coward. So I just made up the lies instead, like having library books due. I had library books in my room all right, but they weren't due for another week.

That day was typical of all my summer days. After lunch, while my dad and the blond bunch sailed and played in the ocean, I spent my day reading. For there is one thing I discovered when I was very young—the kids in the books had to solve problems even worse than mine.

I read anything I could get my hands on—

fiction, nonfiction, comics, even the encyclopedia. It didn't matter—when I was reading I was okay because I wasn't me. My stepsisters called me a bookworm, but hey, it was better than being called a spineless coward afraid of water.

I didn't go to Bobby's birthday party the next weekend. I continued living in silence with my big secret, never expecting things to change. But one June day, not long after that party, I opened the door to Cabin 102 and stumbled into a world beyond compare. Suddenly all my fears and pains spewed out like a shook-up bottle of Coca-Cola.

The only problem is that sometimes thinking about what happened to the person in Cabin 102 hurts more than thinking about drowning.

Bon Voyage

WAS I THE ONLY PERSON on Galveston Island who hated sand? Or maybe it wasn't the sand so much that hot Saturday in June, as the fact that the sand was everywhere I tried to sit. On the bed, on the sofa, on the screened-in back porch, in the seat of Dad's Jeep. Sand—it was the trademark of my stepsisters, Jasmine and Jessica. They swam every morning, every noon, every afternoon, every night, leaving a sandy trail that revealed their erratic movements, like a snail leaves a shiny, sticky trail of slime.

The only place that wasn't covered with a layer of the pale grit was the hammock strung between a cottonwood tree and the corner post of the carport. The hemp had come unraveled and was rotted in the center, so that when I plopped in it my bottom hung down and dragged the ground. It wasn't a pretty sight, but hey, anything was better than hanging around my stepsisters. All they ever wanted to talk about was swimming or the ocean or the beach. You'd think they would be sick of the ocean after living here for the past year. Heck, I was sick of it after visiting my dad for only two weeks. Unfortunately, I still had two more months of summer vacation to go.

Since Bobby never spoke to me anymore, I spent a lot of time alone. I had a pile of library books stacked beside the tree, and was looking forward to a peaceful day of reading. I had just finished chapter ten of *The Farmer's Slaughter,* and the plot was really getting good and gruesome with pitchforks and axes and a runaway combine, when an awful racket filled the air and tore my attention away.

First it was the sound of my stepmother's car horn tooting again and again. That was Vanessa's style, always bubbly and excited about something. I wouldn't have given it much thought, except that when I glanced at the sky I saw the sun hanging over the ocean in the spot that meant it was only two o'clock. You gotta understand, Vanessa was a real workhorse. She not only worked as a P.E. teacher during the school year, she had a job at a sporting goods store during the summer and taught CPR at the YMCA on weekends. She had learned every lifesaving technique known to man—whether you were choking, drowning, having a heart attack, breaking a leg, or getting bit by a rattlesnake, Vanessa knew what to do. That was great, except that she used me and her own kids as guinea pigs every time she learned something new. Vanessa was about the hardest working woman I ever met, except for my mom, of course, who worked *and* took college classes. Anyway, for Vanessa to cut off work and leave the Y early meant something big was up.

Then I heard Jasmine's familiar squeal. I swear, that girl must have been a pig in another life. Or a parrot, maybe. Jasmine was eight and going through that crazy chatterbox stage where she hardly ever paused between paragraphs and charged from one subject right into the next without missing a beat.

I groaned at the thought of my peaceful day being ruined. I really did want to know what happened to the missing head of Farmer Jackson's third wife, Shirlene. I turned the page and started to read again.

But then I heard Jessica's shouts and I couldn't sit still another minute. Jessica was about as tight-lipped as any thirteen-year-old ever came. It practically took an earthquake to get her excited.

I couldn't keep my curiosity down any longer, so I dog-eared the page and snapped the book shut. I wrestled my way out of the hammock and brushed the hemp fibers off the bottom of my shorts. I climbed the steep wooden stairs to the beach house door, and as I looked over the railing made of three-inch-thick anchor rope, I saw Vanessa's car parked at a weird angle, like she had been in a big hurry.

"Dusty! Dusty!" Jasmine's flushed face, with its missing-front-teeth grin, greeted me as I jerked the door open.

"Mom won a trip to the Carrie B. Ann islands." She bounced up and down, making her white-blond hair fall into her eyes.

"To the what?"

"She's *trying* to say Caribbean islands," Jessica explained. With her blond hair slicked back into a ponytail, she looked more like an onion than a girl. She crossed her arms and gave me her usual see-if-I-care stare.

As I stepped inside, I heard my father's voice coming from the living room.

"I don't believe it! You're pulling my leg, Vanny," he was saying as he paged through a colorful brochure. One of the pictures showed a huge ocean liner, its aqua blue swimming pools twinkling on the upper decks like jewels in a white crown.

"Is it true, Charlie?" Jessica asked. I cringed like I always did whenever my stepsister called my dad by his first name.

"Yeah, is it really true, *Va-ness-a?*" I mocked my stepsister, dragging out her mother's name like a piece of saltwater taffy. As usual, Vanessa looked like an ad for exercise equipment, dressed in neat white shorts that accentuated her golden tan and very trim figure.

"Everything looks legal," my dad said. "Yep, I'd say you've won an all-expenses paid cruise for the whole family on the—uh, um"—he cleared his throat, adjusted his black-rimmed glasses, and took on the voice of a TV announcer— "the luxurious *Historia*— the world's most unique ocean liner. You'll take a journey into history in the comfort of your one-of-a-kind cabin. From Spanish galleons to Chinese clippers to the *Queen Mary*, you'll experience the romantic Caribbean Sea firsthand as you visit romantic Cozumel, the exciting Cayman Islands, and historic Jamaica." He lowered the brochure, then grinned. In his favorite khaki shorts, he reminded me of an overgrown Boy Scout.

Vanessa suddenly couldn't hold back another minute. She grabbed each daughter by a hand and all three of them jumped up and down, howling like hound dogs after a rabbit. They laughed and squealed and chanted, "We're going on a sea cruise! We're going on a sea cruise!"

They made so much racket, Jessica's cat got up and left the room. I shook my head, but Dad stood on the sidelines clapping his hands and laughing like they were cute little blond-haired bunnies or something. I stared at him in disbelief. Suddenly a wonderful idea popped into my head. If they went to the Caribbean, then I would get to go back home to Mom and peaceful living. No more chatterbox Jasmine and see-if-I-care Jessica. And best of all, no more sandy beach, no more pounding surf, no more endless green water outside my window reminding me night and day that I was a coward.

"Well, have a great time, folks," I said with a smile. "I'll go call Mom and tell her to come and get me. When are you leaving?"

"Dusty, honey," Vanessa said after she had caught her breath, "of course, you're invited, too. Surely you didn't think we would leave you behind?"

"I can dream, can't I?"

"Russell!" My dad always used my real name when he was ticked off. "I don't want to hear any of your lip today. What kid in the world would turn down the chance to take a free trip to the Caribbean? I visited Jamaica with your mom once. It's paradise. You'll love it."

Yeah, but will I love being in the middle of an ocean? Will I love having water slosh against the ship day and night, like the chant of a sea witch before she grabs me and pulls me down to a watery grave? The very thought of being surrounded by so much water—not just a little creek or kiddie swimming pool but terminally deep water—made my knees begin to shake. A million warning sirens screamed inside my head and my brain cells began a search program to find the best excuse. It stopped under the categories of ocean and boat.

"But, Dad? An ocean voyage? I'll get seasick."

"How do you know that? You've never been on an ocean liner before."

"It can't be much different than a fishing boat. That made me sick as a dog, remember?"

"Don't worry, Dusty," Vanessa said. "I've heard that the ship is so big, it's like walking on land. You'll hardly know you're on the ocean. Besides, you can take some Dramamine every day."

"Great! Now you want me to be a drug addict."

"Russell!" Dad's right eyebrow twisted up.

My brain cells fired like crazy searching the old memory banks for another excuse. The category "ocean" hadn't done the job; "boat" hadn't done the job. How about "Caribbean islands"?

"Hey, I've heard that those islands are full of tropical diseases. You wouldn't want poor little Jasmine to catch something and lose her voice, would you? Heaven forbid that." I put my hands on her skinny shoulders and created a deeply caring expression on my face.

"That's it!" My dad crossed the room, and

I stepped back. "You're going with us. Period. No arguing. No excuses. No lies. I swear sometimes, if you weren't my own son . . ."

"Charlie, honey," Vanessa cooed and put her hand on Dad's arm. He calmed down and didn't finish the sentence, but he didn't have to. I knew what he was thinking. If I weren't his own son, he would drop me off at the nearest loony bin and tell them to throw away the key; he would sail off to a tropical island and never mention my name again; he would send me to juvenile detention; he would throw up in disgust.

An empty ache throbbed in my chest like someone had torn off a piece of my heart. A lump crept up my throat and made my voice sound weird when I spoke.

"Hey, that's cool, Dad," I said with a shrug and a smile. "I would just spoil your trip anyway, so why don't you let me stay here and watch the beach house for you."

A long, ragged sigh slipped from Dad's lips. "Dusty, when are you going to understand that we *want* you to be a part of this family? We *want* you to come with us on trips."

Jasmine, bless her little heart, slipped her sticky, grape Kool-Aid–smeared hand into mine.

"Dusty, I want you to come. It's no fun without you. Please."

I glanced at Jessica. As usual, her arms were crossed and her eyes stared at me with all the warmth of green ice.

"Do I have a choice?" I muttered.

"Well, not really," Dad said. "Your mother is studying for the bar exam and asked me to keep you out of trouble the whole summer. Sorry, looks like you're stuck with us for the cruise."

He tried to ruffle my hair, but I ducked, then charged to my room. While the others giggled and talked about what clothes to buy and how much vacation time my dad had coming from his engineering job, and when to leave, and who would take care of the cat, I pounded my fist into my pillow.

It would be just my luck that this ocean liner was old and leaky, or cursed, or would get sucked up into some alien spacecraft in the Bermuda Triangle. At least that would be better than being pulled down into the ocean.

Suddenly an idea flashed across my mind. I jumped up, grabbed my empty backpack and my library card.

"Later," I called out over my shoulder as I

bounded down the porch steps. "I'm going to the library."

"Not more books," I heard Vanessa say to my dad. "Charlie, that boy always has his nose buried in a book. Why, his whole youth is passing him by."

Well, that's okay with me, lady, I thought as I flipped the kickstand on my bike and pedaled down the road. Better to have my youth pass by with my nose buried in a book than have my youth snuffed out by cold, icy hands pulling me down to the bottom of the sea.

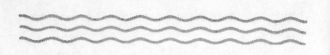

The Historia

THE WATER WAS DEEP, deeper than the Grand Canyon, and I couldn't see the bottom, but I could see a pale silver glow up above me. I knew it was the bottom of the cruise liner. Even though I was underwater, I could hear the band playing one of those very old tunes from the 1940s, and I could hear people laughing and even the clink of champagne glasses.

Why was everyone so happy when I was falling into oblivion? Why hadn't someone yelled "Man overboard" and dropped a life preserver?

When I opened my mouth to cry for help, the water gushed in and I sank even deeper. I could feel something clinging to my legs and when I looked down (somehow the salty seawater didn't burn my eyes), I saw a twenty-foot eel wrapping itself around my left leg. Then I felt something on my shoulder and when I turned around an octopus was sliding its slimy arms around my neck and shoulders. As it shook me like a limp rag, I opened my mouth again to scream.

"Help!" I cried out, jerking my head up from the library table.

"Oh dear!" The librarian took her hand off my shoulder and jumped back. "I'm sorry. I didn't mean to startle you, but the library will be closing in five minutes."

My heart was still working overtime, but I was so relieved to see her red hair and freckled face that I let out a long sigh. I breathed in the familiar musty air of the oldest room of the oldest library in town. The dark, narrow aisles between tall gray shelves loomed like the faces of dear friends. Even the librarian's over-powdered nose was a welcome sight.

"Having a bad dream?" she asked, smiling slightly.

I shrugged and ran my fingers through my hair. "Sorta."

"It wouldn't have anything to do with octopi or eels or sharks, would it?"

My mouth must have dropped to the floor

because suddenly she laughed and pointed to the stacks of books smothering the table. She picked up one called *Terrors of the Deep: True Stories of Sea Monsters and Other Phenomena at Sea.*

"No wonder you're having nightmares." She glanced at the titles of some of the books and read them out loud. *"Mysteries of the Bermuda Triangle, Sharks, The Wreck of the Titanic, The Most Deadly Tidal Waves, Hurricanes—Nature's Fury, Man Overboard . . .* You must be doing research for a summer-school project."

"Not exactly," I said as I snapped shut a three-inch-thick volume called *A Brief History of the Caribbean Islands.* "My family's going on a cruise to the Caribbean. I just want to be prepared."

"Oh, aren't you lucky! I've always wanted to cruise on an ocean liner. The music, the food, the moonlight strolls on the promenade, tropical beaches, handsome foreigners, mysterious women." She clasped her hands together and sighed.

"Yeah, right," I muttered.

As I left, the librarian slipped into my chair and opened one of the books. Slowly she turned the pages, a dreamy look on her face.

That's the way it was all week. Anyone who found out about Vanessa's free vacation turned green with envy. All the guys I knew thought it would be cool to go snorkeling and see coral reefs. Of course, I couldn't let them know how I really felt, so I told them it was going to be a blast and pretended I couldn't wait.

"Yep, I'm going to be sipping on fresh pineapple juice, sitting under a coconut palm, watching those tanned beauties walk by while you guys are back here sweating and smelling dead fish," I told them. "Hey, don't worry, I'll bring you back some souvenirs."

But at home I sang a different tune. I kept reminding Dad and the blond bunch about the terrors at sea. Nothing fazed Jessica. She just turned her head when I read the passages describing shark bites and stingray punctures. She only grunted when I made eerie noises and turned the lights low and read about the ships that vanished from the Bermuda Triangle. But little Jasmine got all spooked and shaky and cried so much that Dad made me stop bringing the books home.

Finally the day of departure arrived, and in spite of the fact that I pretended to have a sudden case of malaria, I found myself at the airport waving good-bye to my mom from the airplane window. She had taken off time from studying to wish me a bon voyage. She had even bought me a new swimsuit and flippers and a snorkel. That really made me feel guilty, since Mom wasn't very rich and had to save every penny. Well, there was no way of getting out of it now. My only hope was for the airplane to have mechanical problems so that we would never make it to Miami in time for the cruise liner's big send-off.

But no such luck. The flight to Florida was smooth and flawless. And not a cloud blemished the perfect blue sky as we checked in at the reception area and then waited for the boarding call on Sunday morning.

Smiling officers, crew, and staff in blinding white uniforms greeted the steady stream of passengers as they shuffled up the gangway. Stewards directed people to their staterooms and bellboys hustled about with luggage.

The lower decks, where passengers slept, had exotic names like Tropicana Deck and Casablanca Deck and Trinidad Deck. Our staterooms were located on the Calypso Deck. We passed down the longest, narrowest halls I had ever seen. The smell of paint and linseed oil crept from every wall and wooden floor, a constant reminder that the ship had been in dry dock for the past year getting a face-lift.

There was a note on our door announcing a safety drill at four o'clock on Lido Deck. Inside the unbelievably neat and clean cabin, I checked the closet to make sure that the bright orange life jackets were safely tucked away. I slipped one on and adjusted the straps.

"You can't wear *that*," Jessica protested, her hands on her narrow hips. "Everyone will think you're crazy."

"Oh yeah?" I retorted. "When the ship starts going down, I won't look so crazy. Then you'll be begging me for this life jacket. But I won't give you one measly inch to hold on to."

Jessica huffed and screamed out the door toward the cabin across the hall where our parents were staying. "Mother! Do I have to share a room with this child?"

Vanessa strolled over, glancing at me, then at Jasmine. "Which child would that be, dear?"

"Him! Look at that life jacket. It's so stupid. Everyone knows how safe these ships are. If he thinks he's wearing that life jacket during the whole cruise, I swear I'll get off right now and go home."

Vanessa leaned over and whispered something into Jessica's ear. I couldn't hear everything she said, but it looked like her lips formed the words "Humor him. He's got problems." I jerked the life jacket off and threw it back into the closet. The ship hadn't even set sail yet, and already my stepsister was a pain. It was going to be a very long eight days.

After dumping our luggage, we took the elevator up to Promenade Deck for the bon voyage party. For years the strolling feet of the idle rich had worn down certain areas of the teak hardwood flooring, but it had been polished to a rich red-brown sheen, as had the long wooden rail that still showed a few nicks and scratches underneath the new coat of varnish.

With all the passengers smiling and laughing as they leaned over the rails and with colorful balloons everywhere, it felt like a big New Year's Eve party. A three-piece steel drum band belted out lively calypso music and stewards kept wine and champagne glasses filled. For the kids, there were soft drinks and pink punch, and for all, a fancy cheese and hors d'oeuvre buffet. On the docks below, friends and relatives of the passengers waved and cheered.

I felt vibrations as the engines accelerated, and then the gentle undulating movement as the *Historia* pulled away. The band churned out a whiny rendition of *Auld Lang Syne*. Confetti and colored streamers shot over the rails and into the air, landing in people's hair and on the shiny clean deck floor. Passengers cheered and laughed and waved good-bye. Jasmine and Jessica blew noisemakers until I thought my ears would burst. When the band switched back to calypso music, the girls hopped around like jumping beans.

Vanessa and Dad smiled and hugged each other and sipped champagne as the skyscrapers and shoreline of Miami gradually grew smaller. They danced to a couple of reggae tunes and forgot that I was alive, so I decided to explore Promenade Deck.

If what you wanted was a piece of history, the *Historia* was the ship for you. It was about as far from modern-looking as you could get. Across the water we could see other cruise liners waiting for passengers or returning from the Caribbean. Those ships were big, multistoried, chunky-looking things, all white and twinkling with glass. They looked more like floating cities than ships.

By comparison, the *Historia* looked long and skinny. Her bottom half was painted black and her smokestacks looked big and heavy enough to topple the ship. The only spot of color was the bright red tarpaulins covering the lifeboats. I know this because while everyone else was dancing or cheering, I was checking out the safety equipment very carefully. I crept as close as I could to the little boats and pulled on lines and tried to figure out how many people would fit inside one of them.

"Don't you worry now, young man," a deep voice with a British accent said behind my back. "This ship is in tip-top condition."

I swung around and saw a friendly smile set in a dark face that might have been a hundred years old. The crisp white uniform, with its polished brass buttons and colorful braid trim, stood out against his dark mahogany-colored skin.

"Have you been working on this ship very long?" I asked.

"Since her maiden voyage back in 1965."

"1965! That's . . . thirty years ago! You've been on this ship that long?"

"Aye-aye, sir." He snapped his long, lean body into attention and saluted with a gloved hand. "I was a young man. Thin as a shoestring back then, I was." He patted his stomach. He still looked thin and straight to me, and I couldn't imagine him being any skinnier.

"I served my apprenticeship on the *Queen Mary* and worked for Cunard Lines for ten years before coming aboard the *Historia*. Met Clark Gable once and one of his lady friends."

"Man, you must be *old*."

The man tilted his head back and laughed gleefully.

"Too old to be rollicking on the sea anymore. That's why this is my last voyage. I'm retiring after this. I'm going back to Jamaica, where I was born. Like a giant sea turtle crawling ashore, I'm returning to the sugar plantation where all my family lived and died." He looked toward the south and a dreamy gaze covered his dark eyes. He looked back down at me. "Excuse me, young sir. Why, where are my manners? My name is Lionel St. Cyr. I'm the chief steward of Calypso Deck." He pronounced his last name like the word *sincere*.

"Hey, we're staying on that deck. Glad to meet you. I'm Dusty."

"Why, you look as clean as a shark's tooth to me," he said with a wink as he shook my hand. When he saw my grimace, he cocked his head to one side. "I think maybe you've heard many a joke about your name, haven't you?"

I shrugged. "Doesn't matter to me. It's better than my real name."

"Well, if you ever need anything during your cruise, young Dusty, just ask for Lionel." He gave a reserved bow and walked away, tall and straight as a palm tree. As I watched him strolling across the deck, I had a sudden thought.

"Lionel," I called out and ran after him. "Have you ever had to use one of those lifeboats? Has the *Historia* ever had to evacuate, or had any kind of problems? This ship is *really* old, you know."

Lionel's face took on an expression of indignation. "*Old* doesn't mean incapable. Many things get better with age."

"Sure, I know that. But is there a chance something is all rusted up, like an engine part? Maybe rust is eating a hole in the hull along a seam line."

"The *Historia* has spent the past year in dry dock, getting completely renovated and modernized."

I heaved a sigh. "Sure, sure, I read all that in the brochures. But you still didn't answer my question. Has this ship ever had to use those lifeboats or had any kinds of problems in the past?"

Lionel glanced left and right and behind him, then leaned so close I could see the gray stubble of whiskers on his chin. He lowered his voice to a whisper.

"Young man, you don't want to know."

"But, has anything happened? Anything dangerous?"

He placed a long, bony finger to his lips. "Talking 'bout it only brings more bad luck. It's best if you don't ask so many questions 'bout certain things. All those deaths were just accidents."

"Deaths?" I felt a shiver travel up and down my body as he walked away. *Great,* I thought. *No wonder Vanessa won a free cruise. We're on a death ship.*

Captain Ahab
Slept Here

AFTER THE BAND FINISHED UP and Miami
had faded out of sight, most of the passengers
strolled the decks, exploring the facilities. The
Historia was not a superliner that housed three
thousand passengers, but she wasn't small, either. The brochure said she carried up to one
thousand passengers and had four hundred
staff and crew. And believe me, I think all of
them were strolling the decks at the same time
that first afternoon at sea.

My parents methodically visited every restaurant, lounge, bar, and sports facility, taking
one deck at a time. My stepsisters giggled and
squealed and ran in every direction, getting totally lost. I kept running across them at every
turn, first in the video game room, then up on

Lido Deck where some white-haired women were already playing shuffleboard and a few couples were in the swimming pool. Later I ran into Jasmine at the ice-cream parlor, and not five minutes later I bumped into Jessica coming out of the theater. As expected, I saw Vanessa checking out the exercise equipment, sauna, and indoor Jacuzzi in the health spa. My dad, not able to leave his engineering brain behind, looked at every beam and brace and knocked on walls and signed up for a tour of the engine room.

I finally reached the top deck, Verandah Deck, where a red jogging track circled around a penthouse lounge. As I looked out over the ocean, I saw the Florida Keys off the starboard side and blue-green water ahead of us as far as the eyes could see. Now, don't get me wrong, I don't mind heights—I'd rather be on a mountaintop than any place on earth—but all of that water gave me the willies. The ship was traveling at her cruising speed of nineteen knots now, creating a strong breeze that chilled me in spite of the sunshine. I gripped the stair rail and inched my way back down to Lido Deck where the ship's ten-foot-deep pool was located. It was at the stern of the ship, with a café and bar sheltering it from the strong wind. The four-foot-deep pool was one deck below.

My knees felt a little shaky when I finally returned to my cabin and flopped on the tiny roll-out bed. I hadn't been there ten minutes when the door burst open and my stepsisters announced that it was time for the safety drill. We grabbed our bright orange life jackets from the closet and assembled on Lido Deck with about a hundred other passengers from our deck.

The first mate droned out the statistics of the *Historia,* her tonnage, her length and width and draft, number of boilers, and her cruising speed. Five crew members passed out maps of the ship and emergency instructions, then demonstrated how to put on the life jackets and how to use the lifeboat assigned to us. The first mate gave instructions for exiting our cabins and showed us how to use the fire extinguishers. He also showed us a square glass box. Others like it were strategically located on each deck. Inside the box was a big red switch that, when flipped, let out a piercing blast that could be heard all over the ship. As soon as he flipped it back, the noise ceased.

The passengers laughed nervously and joked, but I made sure I learned exactly where our lifeboat was located, and I memorized the locations of all the glass boxes before returning to our staterooms.

Just as the brochures had described, each cabin had a motif from a different time period. My parents' room was a replica of a stateroom aboard the luxury liner *Queen Mary* in the 1930s, with satin bedcovers, Tiffany lamps, a rounded mirror on the built-in dresser, and those old-fashioned velvet chairs like you always see in antique stores. It was pretty boring stuff, except for the commode. You flushed it by pulling a ceramic handle on the end of a chain, and the tank was up in the air instead of low beside the seat. The ceramic handles on the bathtub were huge, too, and the water gushed out of the faucets like Niagara Falls.

As for my cabin, there were some good points and some bad points. The worst thing was that I had to share it with Jessica and Jasmine. Each girl had a twin bed covered with a deep blue bedspread tucked in so tight you could break a toe on it. The headboards looked like the steering wheels on an old schooner. The end table lamps were replicas of oil-burning brass lanterns from the 1800s. I had to sleep on the roll-out cot. It was tiny and the mattress was thin, but I didn't mind. It was a small price to pay for being across the room from my stepsisters.

The neatest thing in the room was a giant whaling harpoon on the wall. Right above it hung a huge picture of the great white whale, Moby Dick, with Captain Ahab stuck on its back, tangled up in harpoon lines. The expression on the captain's face wasn't exactly the kind of thing you like to see before bedtime. The black eyes and the look of horror gave me the willies. And as luck would have it, my cot faced the painting, so that when I lay down, I had a perfect view of old Ahab.

The first thing the girls did, after bouncing on their beds, was to look out the old-fashioned round porthole. I took a quick peek, and my heart wanted to flip over when I saw nothing but deep, dark water. My stomach had a sudden sinking feeling and I had to sit on the bed. While I was ashore, the ship had been just a piece of lifeless machinery, but now I felt like it was an entity and I was its prisoner. Even the gentle sway of the ship reminded me of someone breathing.

"Come on, Dusty, let's go to the swimming pool," Jasmine said, as she dumped the contents of her suitcase on her bed and rummaged for her favorite swimsuit. She had dozens of them, but she always ended up wearing the same one, a little pink thing with yellow polka dots.

"And I want to go join that special club they have for eight- to twelve-year-olds," Jasmine continued. "They're going to have activities all day long every day. I can't wait for the scavenger hunt, can you? And then there is a pirate treasure hunt, too. And a Coke party and an ice-cream party and a pizza pig-out. And a costume party, and a mock Olympics competition, and a poster contest. Everyone seventeen and under is supposed to meet by the pool in thirty minutes to learn who their counselors are and to break up into different age clubs."

She grabbed a sheet of blue paper from the dresser. "Here's today's Daily Schedule. Our cabin stewardess puts a new schedule under the door every night so we can have it first thing in the morning and can plan our day. See." She waved the sheet under my nose. "It says right here, five P.M.—children meet on Lido Deck by the deep pool. Did you know they have two pools—one deep and one not so deep? Why do they call it Lido Deck? What does *Lido* mean, Dusty?"

I groaned and rolled over on my stomach,

trying to shut off the chatter. I watched Jessica, calm as always, carefully remove items from her suitcase and neatly place them in the dresser drawers or hang them in the tiny closet. When she came out of the bathroom dressed in an ever-so-mature bikini, I chuckled under my breath.

"Here," I said, tossing her two fresh oranges from the complimentary fruit basket on the dresser. "You'll need these to stuff inside your swimsuit."

Jessica turned her icy green gaze on me, ground her teeth a second, then grabbed her beach towel.

"You are so immature," she said, slamming the cabin door behind her.

"What?" I said to Jasmine, who had turned to me, her hands on her tiny hips.

"Oh, you men are all alike," she said with a sigh, then leaped on my bed. "Aren't you going to change into your swim trunks? We've got to hurry. Come on, Dusty." She tugged my arm, but I stood up and headed for the bathroom, the only place I knew that would be safe from her never-ending chatter.

"You go on," I said. "My stomach is doing flip-flops right now. I'm going to put on a seasickness patch and lie down a minute before I go swimming." I rubbed my tummy and rolled my eyes, then darted to the bathroom, slammed the door, and made pukey noises until I heard the cabin door close and all was quiet inside.

What I had said wasn't that much of a lie. My stomach didn't feel so great. The thought of all that ocean out there was making my head spin. I stepped to the tiny vanity sink and leaned over to wash my face, then turned the cold water handle. Nothing came out. I tried the hot water handle; still nothing came out.

"Oh, great," I mumbled. Maybe the plumber had forgotten to turn on the water after the renovations. An eight-day cruise with no water would be very interesting. I turned around and opened the door to leave. Suddenly water shot from the faucet, hitting the sink and splashing all over the floor and my shirt. I frantically spun the cold water handle. Nothing! Out of desperation I turned the hot water handle. Suddenly they both stopped.

"This is some renovation," I said out loud. I turned the handles again, and this time they worked perfectly. As I changed shirts and wiped up the mess with a towel, I wondered if I should tell Lionel about the malfunction. On the other hand, maybe I'd let Jessica discover the wonderful faucet for herself. I grinned as I tossed my suitcase on my bed and began unpacking. I guess something out there was paying me back for having mean thoughts, because as I rummaged through clothes and shoes and underwear, I discovered that I had left behind the most important things in the world.

"Where are my books?" I groaned. I dug through the suitcase again, then pilfered through Jasmine's pile of junk, too. All the books that I had especially picked to get me through this ordeal had been accidentally left on the kitchen table.

I slapped my forehead in disgust. Now what was I going to do? How could I exist without books? Without stories about other kids' problems, I would have nothing to think about but my own misery.

I plopped down on the bed. "This old tub better have a library, or else I don't even want to think about the next eight days," I muttered to Captain Ahab. He just leered back at me with a smirk on his face, so I pulled the pillow over my head and fell asleep.

When I woke up, the room was dark except for dim light coming through the porthole. I flipped on the nearest lamp, but nothing happened. I tried all three lamps, but none of them worked. I could have sworn that they were on before I went to sleep.

"Another example of fine craftsmanship," I muttered.

I was starving, so when my stepsisters burst in and said it was time to change for dinner, I hopped up and got ready. There were several places to eat on the ship, from fancy restaurants to casual cafés to hamburger joints on the outside deck. But for dinner in the grand Paradise Dining Room, no shorts or swimsuits were allowed; it was a ship rule. Floor-to-ceiling windows gave a view of the ocean in all directions, making the room seem endless. Waiters in white gloves bustled everywhere, filling wine glasses, bringing freshly baked bread, helping women into their chairs.

I must admit the food was out of this world. They were serving one of those buffets on a block-long table covered with every kind of fruit and vegetable and bread and meat in the world. Assistant chefs in crisp white uniforms and tall white hats stood behind the meat board, slicing succulent prime rib of beef, or pork roast, or turkey. Passengers piled up food on their plates as if they had been stranded on a deserted island for a year.

"Oh dear," Vanessa said as we waited in line. "The brochures never told us that we could expect to gain twenty pounds on the cruise."

"Why do you think they have an exercise room and aerobics classes and a jogging track?" my dad kidded.

The meal passed quickly, with everyone announcing his or her plans for the rest of the night. My dad couldn't wait to hit the blackjack tables and roulette wheel on Casino Deck. Vanessa wanted to work out on the exercise equipment, soak in a Jacuzzi, and then get a Swedish massage before dressing up for the captain's cocktail party.

After dinner, out on the verandah of Calypso Deck, I played a few card games with Jasmine, killing time until eight o'clock when all the welcome parties started. Three separate parties were going on—one for adults, one for teens, and one for kids twelve and under. I tried all three of them but didn't feel right anywhere. The adult party was no fun; passengers were waiting in line to be introduced to the captain and to have their pictures taken with him. Most people stood around guzzling down cocktails. I tried the teen party next, but they treated me like a bothersome kid. They danced like maniacs on the disco floor to loud music that hurt my eardrums and made my head throb. Jessica told me all twelve-year-olds had to go to the younger kids' party. But when I visited the little kids, I felt like a hippo in the middle of a party for miniature pigs. They only wanted to play games that required a lot of jumping and running and limbo dancing.

After my fill of cake and cookies and punch, I finally gave up and returned to my stateroom. The first thing I noticed was that all the lamps were brightly beaming again. The wiring on the ship must really be faulty, I thought. Now I knew I had to find Lionel tomorrow.

The girls came in around eleven o'clock, exhausted from chasing counselors up and down every deck all evening and from dancing all night at the welcome parties. They fell asleep fast. But I couldn't sleep at all. Maybe it was the nap I had taken earlier. Maybe it was the fear in Captain Ahab's eyes as he glared at me from the painting. Light from a three-quarter moon streamed through the porthole, hitting old Ahab smack in the face and making the painting look alive. I swore I could see the great white whale lumbering through the ocean, his waterspout spewing foam fifty feet into the air. I could hear Captain Ahab's cries of pain and horror as Moby Dick pulled him down again and again into the icy water.

I swallowed hard and pulled the blanket up to my chin. I closed my eyes and turned my back on the painting, but that only made it worse. I could almost feel the coldness and darkness of the black water. My bed even felt like the slick back of an angry whale.

I heard the swish of the ocean and wind outside the porthole and felt the gentle sway of the *Historia,* almost as if she were alive and breathing softly as she moved through the darkness. I thought about the ocean surrounding us, dark and deeper than a mountain is tall. Anyone who fell overboard would never stand a chance of survival. I imagined the horror of falling, falling deeper and deeper, waiting for the water to swallow me up. I had never felt so lonely and alone in my life. Surely I was the only person out of fifteen hundred aboard who was afraid of water.

My body began to tremble and sweat trickled down my temples and chest. I should have tossed the covers off, but I couldn't. Somehow I knew that if I ever removed the covers, I would be exposing myself to whatever horror lurked in the dark room. I wanted to scream, but I didn't dare wake my step-sisters. So I lay there, shaking and sweating, listening to the alarm clock ticking, and wishing the night would go away.

Suddenly I heard a noise. It seemed to be coming from the cabin next door—Cabin 102. I strained my ears until I heard the sound again. It was someone crying. Not the cry of a little baby or kid that was mad or hungry. The cry was a frightened whimper, not too loud, and full of sadness.

I sat up and tiptoed across the tiny state-room. My sisters breathed the deep, slow breath of peaceful sleep. I pressed my ear to the wall and listened. The crying was continuous now, so sad it almost tore my heart out. It was definitely a girl crying. Not a woman, not a little kid, but a girl.

I tried to remember who was in Cabin 102, but I drew a blank. I couldn't recall seeing any-one go in or out of that room, and I had not heard any door slamming or toilets flushing since I had been aboard. I did remember one thing—the door to Cabin 102. It was one of those ancient Spanish types—heavy, dark wood carved with vines and flowers, topped with a fancy brass handle that had an elaborate cross etched in its base. The brochure said that some of the staterooms were replicas of Spanish galleons from the sixteenth century. Cabin 102 was probably decorated in that style.

As I leaned against the wall, I wondered why the girl was alone. Maybe her parents were still at the casino or dancing at the disco. Her sobs were so bitter, I could almost feel them coming through the wall. They seemed to grab my heart and shake my body. Finally, I couldn't take it another minute. I tapped lightly on the wall. The crying stopped.

"Hey, little girl, don't cry," I whispered. "I know you're alone and scared. Maybe you hate the ocean and you want to be back home in your own safe, cozy bed. I'll bet you don't have any friends, either. But don't worry, you'll be all right. Go back to sleep now and I promise I'll visit you tomorrow. We'll make it through this cruise together."

I touched the wall, and of course it's silly to think this, but I swear I felt her placing her hand against the wall, too. Her hand was cool, soft, and light like a butterfly's wing. "Good," I whispered. "Now go to sleep."

I slid back into my bed. She didn't cry again and I felt good inside, as if I'd just saved someone's life or something like that. I started imagining what she looked like and wondering how old she was and what her name was. As I imagined what I would say to her and what we would do tomorrow, I fell into a deep, peaceful sleep.

Cabin 102

I WOKE UP the next morning, Monday, to the sound of the telephone ringing. Jasmine and Jessica both dived for it, but Jessica won the race.

"It's for me," she snapped at her little sister, then spoke into the mouthpiece in a voice as sweet as honey. "Hello. Oh, hi, Brandon. No, you didn't wake me up."

Jasmine rolled her eyes and plopped on my bed.

"Brandon is a guy she met last night at the welcome party. She says he's a hunk." Jasmine was holding a new daily schedule that had miraculously appeared under the door sometime during the night. She pored over the listing of the day's activities, then heaved a heavy sigh.

"There's just not enough time in the day to do everything."

I yawned and rubbed my eyes. A quick peek out the porthole showed that we were in the middle of the ocean, with no land in sight. The water had turned azure blue, not like the murky green waves that splashed on the beach at Galveston.

"What are you going to do today, Dusty?" Jasmine asked, and handed me the blue sheet.

"Well, let's see. Sunrise tai chi on Verandah Deck. Walk-a-Mile organized walking around the track. Aqua exercises in the deep pool at eight o'clock. Now that sounds like Vanessa's kind of schedule."

"I bet you can't figure out what Charlie is going to do this morning."

I glanced over the schedule again. Golf lessons, tango lessons, bridge lessons, financial seminar, computer lecture, bingo game. "Ah, this has to be it," I said. "Psychic readings at ten A.M." I tossed the blue sheet back at Jasmine.

She squealed triumphantly. "No. He's shooting skeets off the end of the ship. Dusty, what are skeets? Are they little birds? I hope he doesn't kill any. I think it's terrible to shoot little birds just for fun."

I tossed a pillow at her face.

"Ugh! Give your motormouth a break." I jumped up and ran to the bathroom. When the phone rang again, I heard Jessica's "hello" pour out of her throat like honey. "Oh, it's you, Mom. Okay, bye." She slammed the receiver and shouted, "Mom says to meet her for breakfast on Lido Deck in fifteen minutes. She's almost finished exercising."

I'll say one thing for the *Historia*, the cooks knew how to put out a great spread. We could have eaten at a closed-in restaurant, but the buffet by the pool was more convenient. Everything you could imagine was there—fresh fruit, eggs, bacon, sausage, ham, steak, pancakes, waffles, muffins, jellies and jams, fruit drinks, coffee, milk.

"Wow," Vanessa squealed as she joined us, a towel wrapped around her neck. "Can you believe all this food?" In spite of all the scrumptious choices, she placed some fruit and half an English muffin on her plate. She was still wearing her skintight aerobics outfit, the one that emphasized her small waist and tight, hard muscles. Tiny beads of perspiration glistened on her forehead.

"Ah, forget about your figure for one week, Vanny," Dad said as he walked up dressed in khaki shorts, a pink-and-yellow Hawaiian shirt that hurt your eyes to look at, and a khaki hat. He piled on the food until it was a miracle the plate didn't crack. Jessica followed her mother's lead and selected fruit and a bowl of whole-grain cereal with low-fat milk. Jasmine grabbed a cinnamon roll and a Danish.

"Did you shoot any skeets?" I asked as I balanced my plates.

"Yeah, I managed to hit seven out of ten. Not bad for a nearsighted old coot, huh?"

"Poor little skeets," Jasmine whined. "You're so mean, Charlie."

"What?" Dad's brows shot up. "Honey, skeets aren't alive. They're just pieces of clay."

"Oh, Dusty, why didn't you tell me?" She punched my arm, and I hurried off to look for a table. All the tables by the pool were taken, so I climbed the steps to Verandah Deck and put my food down, then waved at Dad. The table overlooked the deep swimming pool on the deck below. The aqua exercisers were just beginning, mostly older women with rubber swimming caps crammed over their heads, making their noses look bigger than normal. The sky was unbelievably blue and clear, and there was nothing but blue water meeting blue sky, broken only by specks of white foam on the swells. The air was cool and fresh, tinged with the smell of salt. It reminded me of being at the giant aquarium at the zoo.

While we were eating, I noticed some water stains on my dad's shirt.

"Dad, how'd you get so wet?" I asked as I tore into my food.

Vanessa broke out in laughter. "The water faucet attacked him this morning."

"It wasn't that funny," my dad grumbled.

"Ours was acting up last night, too," I said. "I'm going to tell Lionel first thing this morning."

"Who's Lionel?" Dad asked.

"He's the chief steward of Calypso Deck. He's really neat. He was born on a sugar plantation in Jamaica about sixty years ago. He served his apprenticeship on the *Queen Mary*. He shook Clark Gable's hand."

"Really?" Vanessa's eyebrows shot up and I knew she was thinking that this was just another of my tall tales.

"I met Lionel yesterday while you guys were dancing on the deck. He told me to get him if we needed any help."

"Well, that's good, son," Dad commented.

"Why don't you find Lionel right after breakfast and tell him our bathroom fixtures are acting up. And our lights flickered off and on a few times, too. Must be a loose wire. That happens sometimes after remodeling."

I smiled and started eating again. At least Dad was pretending to believe me, even if he didn't. It was a start. If the rest of the cruise could go so smoothly, I'd be happy. But, no, I guess with stepsisters like mine things can never go smoothly. I noticed that Jasmine had been studying my face all during breakfast, kind of the way a dog or cat sometimes just sits there staring at its master. Suddenly she put her fork down and her face clouded up.

"Dusty?" she said. "Why were you crying last night?"

"What?" I nearly choked on my French toast and had to gulp down some orange juice. "What are you talking about?"

"Dusty, were you crying?" Vanessa's face took on that worried mother expression and she stopped eating.

"No, I wasn't crying," I said.

"Yes, you were," Jessica joined in. "I heard you, too."

"You're crazy," I protested as I got up.

"Russell, sit back down," Dad insisted.

"Now, if you were crying, we need to talk about it. I knew you were reluctant to come on this cruise, but I didn't think you were that upset."

I heaved a sigh and ran my fingers through my hair. "Geez! I just told you I wasn't crying. Why don't you ever believe me?"

"When you start telling the truth on a regular basis, maybe I will start believing you. Trust isn't something given away, young man. You have to earn it."

My face must have turned ten shades of purple.

"Charlie, *shh*," Vanessa whispered, putting her hand over his. "Dusty, honey, if it wasn't you crying, then who was it?" Vanessa sounded like she was talking to a four-year-old who'd just broken her favorite sugar bowl.

I tried to swallow my indignation. "It was some kid in the cabin next door. A girl, I think. She sounded scared and lonely. I heard her, too."

"Oh, brother," Jessica said, rolling her green eyes. "It was not a *girl*. It was *you*."

"Was not!" I shouted.

"Russell! Don't yell. Sit down and finish your breakfast."

I plopped down in the chair and slurped

the rest of the orange juice, hiding my face in the glass.

"May I please be excused?" I asked as I put the glass down.

"All right," Dad said, "but—"

I didn't give him time to finish his sentence. I shoved the chair back and ran down the steps from Verandah Deck.

I roamed the decks at least half an hour, trying to cool down. On Promenade Deck, honeymooners clinging to each other strolled by or leaned over the rail, smiling and pointing at a school of dolphins. I really wanted to look at them, too, so I inched to the rail and held on to it with a death grip. I watched the beautiful, sleek, gray animals frolicking in the blue water. They seemed so carefree and happy. They loved the water like I loved solid ground. Envy shot through me. If only I had been born a dolphin, all my problems would be over. I would never have to make up excuses about being afraid of water and my dad would have no reason to doubt my word.

As I walked across Trinidad Deck, I heard a walkie-talkie crackle, then saw Lionel's tall, skinny form going into a storage room.

"Lionel!" I shouted, then trotted up to him and stood in the door.

"Well, hello, young Dusty. How are you this morning?" he asked. I watched him rummage around inside the room, lifting towels and boxes filled with tiny bars of soaps and miniature bottles of shampoo.

"What are you looking for? Can I help?"

"Why certainly. I'm looking for a silver tea setting. We have several British passengers on this cruise—a group of salesmen who won this trip for selling some sort of gadget. We've run short of tea sets. I recall seeing an extra tea service tucked away. I thought it was in here."

I lifted cartons of paper towels and toilet tissue until we had searched every corner of that small room.

"Oh, bother!" Lionel said, scratching his graying head. "I suppose it's in one of the other storage rooms."

"I'll help you look for it."

"Thank you, I appreciate the offer. But don't you have some activities to attend? Isn't the treasure hunt starting in a few minutes? I saw a motley crew of peg-legged rapscallions hiding in the stairwell a few minutes ago."

I shrugged. "I don't care about that stuff. I don't like being outside. I'd rather be inside, where I can't see the ocean."

"*Hmm.*" Lionel's dark eyes looked into

mine and suddenly I felt like he was reading my mind. "A boy who doesn't like the ocean on a sea cruise. Now, that's highly unusual. Well, then you are most welcome to help me search for the missing tea service."

"Great!" I watched him lock the door with a big ring of jangling keys, and then walked with him to another storage room. We searched this one inside out, too, with no luck. All the time we walked and searched, Lionel told me about himself. He was a bit of a chatterbox, like Jasmine, but I didn't mind. Everything he said was fascinating. Like what it was like living on a sugar plantation as a child. He and his father and brothers would cut sugarcane until their hands bled, and until they dropped from exhaustion. His mother died from a fever and his father died from hard labor. Lionel had decided he wasn't going to be stuck on the plantation all his life and die like his father, so at age thirteen he ran away to Kingston. He stowed away on a boat that ended up in England.

"It was a lucky day when they took me on as a cabin boy on the *Queen Mary*," he said as he locked up the third storage room. "Back then it was very fashionable to have an exotic black servant like me."

"You—exotic?"

"Why, certainly, mon. Can't you tell?" His usual stiff British accent suddenly turned into a deep, jolly Jamaican accent. He stuck his chin in the air, then broke into a riotous laugh.

I couldn't help but laugh, too. As I followed him down the long corridor that led toward my own cabin, I suddenly remembered last night.

"Lionel, I almost forgot to tell you something. The water faucet in my bathroom is acting crazy. And the lamps are going off and on when they want to. The same thing's happening in my parents' cabin, too." I pointed across the hall.

Lionel suddenly got very quiet and bit his lip.

"I see. And is that all? Is anything else strange happening?"

"No, I don't think so. Well, there was this girl crying last night, but that doesn't have anything to do with faucets and electricity. By the way, can you tell me who's in Cabin 102, or is that privileged information? I don't need her name, but can you tell me what the girl staying in there looks like? How old is she?"

Lionel's face looked very funny. The dark

mahogany color turned kind of gray and his eyes got wider.

"I assure you, young Dusty, you did not hear a girl in Cabin 102. There is no one in there."

"No one? You mean it's empty? I thought I heard you say earlier that this cruise was completely booked up."

"That is correct. But we never book Cabin 102. Come along, I'll show you what I mean. That was my next stop anyway in the never-ending search for the missing tea service."

We continued down the long corridor and stopped in front of Cabin 102, with its elaborately carved oak door and fancy brass handle. Lionel rattled the keys and slipped one into the lock. When he opened the heavy door, a blast of cold air sent shivers running up my spine and chill bumps rose like little mountains all over my arms.

"Yuck, it smells funny in here."

"That's from all the old items being stored here," Lionel explained. "This is where we put extra furniture and all kinds of odds and ends that we don't use anymore, things too good to throw away."

My eyes scanned the room. Junk was

stacked at weird angles everywhere—chairs, paintings, coffee tables, books, lamps, shuffleboard sticks, toys, a couple of mattresses.

"Whew!" I held my nose and fanned the air with my hand. "Why is all this stuff here? I mean, this looks like it used to be a big stateroom, not a storage room. With that fancy-looking door, I figured this room would be pretty neat."

"Oh, it was very la-di-da in its day. The cruise line spared no expense with the doors to the cabins, as you can tell. This one is an exact replica of the door on a Spanish galleon that really existed. Her name was the *Estrella Vespertina*—that means 'Evening Star' in Spanish. She sank in 1511 in a hurricane. She was discovered by treasure hunters in the early 1950s. The door had rotted away, of course, but the brass handle was still there. That's the very handle you see on this door."

"This handle?"

I touched the shiny metal and felt something weird run up my arm right to my heart and then to my brain. For a minute I couldn't breathe, and I thought I heard voices screaming and crying in Spanish. I couldn't let go for several seconds and had to jerk my hand away.

I rubbed my fingers as if they had been shot full of electricity.

"Man," I muttered, and wiggled my fingers.

"Ah, there is my prodigal child," Lionel exclaimed from one of the corners where he was stooped over an old dresser. He turned around, his face beaming and his hands holding a tarnished silver tea service on an oblong silver tray.

"I don't remember putting it in here, but that's typical. A lot of strange things happen in this room."

"What do you mean?"

Lionel glanced around the room and put his long, bony finger to his lips.

"I'll tell you later," he whispered.

"But—"

"*Shh*, later. When we're not in here." His eyes swept over the room again before he flipped the light switch and closed the heavy oak door.

Lionel rubbed the teapot with his brilliantly white handkerchief, and I carried the sugar bowl, creamer, and tray as we walked down the corridor.

"I don't understand, Lionel," I said. "If the

cruise line went to so much expense and trouble to get that fancy door and antique handle, why is Cabin 102 being used as a storage room? Isn't that bad business?"

"Bad business? Yes, you could say that."

"Then why is it closed up?"

"Now, you don't want to bother your head with silly rumors and such, young Dusty. It'll only make you worry for nothing."

"Rumors? Tell me, Lionel. Don't I have a right to know? I'm staying in the room next to Cabin 102."

"All right, but don't tell anyone that I told you this. Cabin 102 has been nothing but bad luck since the maiden voyage of this ship. Lights don't work half the time, the water faucet goes off and on, the porthole comes open even after it's been locked. It's always cold, even when the air conditioner is turned off. We had so many complaints, that we finally had to stop using it."

"Oh, is that all? I thought it was something really spooky."

Lionel glanced around, then took my arm and led me to the stairwell at the end of the hall. He sat on the top step and pulled me down beside him.

"Now, this is strictly confidential," he

whispered. His long, narrow face looked eerie in the yellow light of the stairwell. "I would be dismissed if the captain found out I told you. Swear to me that you'll never tell anyone."

I gulped and nodded. "I swear."

"There have been unexplained deaths in that cabin, too."

"Deaths?"

"In 1966 a member of the Swedish royal family had a heart attack in that room."

"A heart attack? Is that all? That happens every day."

"Right you are. Then in 1978 a rock 'n' roll singer, Milby James, died from a drug overdose. He was the lead singer for that British rock group the Puffins."

"Well, what else is new? That's not so unusual."

"I see. Young Dusty isn't easily impressed." Lionel rubbed his chin, then held up a bony finger and leaned forward until his face was only inches from mine. "In 1985 an Arabian oil baron's cousin was traveling incognito with his mistress. She killed him in a lover's quarrel."

I swallowed hard. "How'd he die?"

"Gunshot wound. One clean, neat shot through the heart."

"Oh, man, is that all? I thought you were going to say decapitation or dismemberment or disemboweling."

Lionel raised one eyebrow and pursed his lips as he leaned back. "I see. You've been watching a lot of American telly. Death doesn't scare you, then. You're an old hand at it, *hmm?*"

I shrugged. "No, but it's just that all those things you said were, well, ordinary deaths. The way you acted, I thought it was going to be something really, really weird. You know what I mean?"

Lionel nodded, then rose to his feet. "I know precisely what you mean." I saw a hurt look in his eyes and suddenly felt like a worm.

"But I guess when you think of three deaths in one cabin, that is strange. Thanks for telling me, Lionel. That's impressive, really it is," I said in my most cheerful voice.

Lionel didn't reply as he walked down the stairs. I watched the top of his gray head until he was gone, then I sat back down and began thinking about what Lionel had said.

Mechanical problems weren't scary. And the deaths Lionel mentioned weren't scary. Besides, none of that explained the girl crying last night. Maybe she had gotten locked inside the room accidentally. But surely she had finally gotten out okay, or else we would have found her still in the room. Knowing that the room was empty had not satisfied my curiosity. If anything, the girl was more of a mystery now than ever. Obviously she had been there. Jessica and Jasmine had heard her crying, too.

As I got up and climbed the stairs, a new thought leaped into my head. Suppose she had been in that room after all but didn't want us to find her. Maybe Lionel and I hadn't seen her because she was hiding.

"That's it!" I said out loud. "She's a stowaway!"

The Evening Star

THE SHIP WAS NOT DUE to dock at the first port of call, Cozumel, until noon, so I passed the time messing around. I played a few games in the video arcade, but that was boring because I was the only one there. Most of the older guys were swimming or at a scheduled activity. It seemed like every few minutes a youth counselor leading a group of little kids or teens would come tromping up the stairs or pass in front of me. I had already seen the movie showing in the theater, and browsing in the gift shop was boring because I was saving all my money for souvenirs and stuff from the islands.

As I strolled along the promenade, I heard the pulsating strains of tango music from the ballroom, where mostly women passengers and gentlemen hosts learned to strut, glide, dip, and turn dramatically across the polished wooden dance floor. It was only ten o'clock in the morning, but as I passed by the casino I heard the distinctive crunch of a slot machine handle being pulled, then the whir of the slots turning, then the tinkle of quarters spilling out of its mouth. The player picked up the change and immediately fed it back into the machine.

I saw my parents seated inside a lecture hall, listening to every word that came from the mouth of a middle-aged staff member explaining about all the shopping places in Cozumel and in Cancun, a few hours away on the Yucatán Peninsula. Another staff member explained the various sightseeing spots on the island, as well as day-long snorkeling excursions to Playa del Carmen or bus excursions to major Mayan ruins at ancient cities with names like Tulum and Cobá. Just hearing the man lecture about the ancient people and the Spaniards who brought death and destruction made me want to find out more.

"What I need is a good book," I whispered to myself as I stood on the deck, feeling lost. Now would be the perfect time to read about the *Estrella Vespertina,* if she had really existed. Lionel might have been pulling my leg, but there was only one way to find out.

The gift shop cashier told me where to find the ship's library. It was tucked away at the far end of Tropicana Deck, in a quiet, secluded spot. The library was divided into two sections—hardback and paperback. Most of the paperbacks were mysteries or romances or thrillers, while the hardbacks were mostly current bestsellers and travel books. A sunken, sun-drenched lounge under an atrium area, with plush chairs and potted plants, divided the library in half. Sunshine streamed in on the only patron sitting there.

I browsed around until I found the history section. It consisted of a clump of books, old and never used by the look of the dust settled on them. One was called *Spanish Galleons of the Caribbean;* another was *Treasure Hunting in the Caribbean.* I also found two more thick Caribbean history books. I checked them out and started back to my room.

I had just turned the corner when I bumped into my stepmother. She had changed into a one-piece white swimsuit that hugged her trim figure and emphasized her golden tan.

"Dusty, we've been looking all over for you!" Vanessa exclaimed.

"I was in the library."

Vanessa sighed. "Honey, why aren't you playing with the other boys and girls? You need to get some fresh air and sunshine. Why don't you put those musty old books away until bedtime. Get some exercise. The swimming pools look fantastic. The girls are there right now."

"Great idea," I lied. "I was just on my way to my room to change into my swim trunks." I forced a smile and watched Vanessa's eyes light up.

"Good. I'll tell the girls you'll join them in a minute."

I kept my word and changed into my swimming trunks. Vanessa was right about needing some fresh air. But that didn't mean that I was going to get into the water. I stuffed the library books into a canvas tote, slipped on some thongs, and took the elevator to Lido Deck.

It was a bright, sunny day with a brilliant blue sky. The gentle breeze felt great on my face and the smell of the salty ocean wasn't bad, if you liked that sort of thing. It looked like half the ship's passengers were sprawled in sun-splashed lounge chairs or swimming in the pools or hanging out at the Kon-Tiki Bar on Lido Deck.

If you leaned over the rail, you could see the shallow pool one deck below. A counselor wearing a silly duck-shaped hat was supervising water games for the youngest kids since they were not allowed in the deeper pool without a parent. But a few of the older kids, like Jasmine and Jessica, were splashing around in the adult pool. Some of them were practicing for the mock Olympics competition.

I spread my beach towel over a lounge chair wedged between an old man covered with liver spots and a fat lady with a blanket pulled up to her neck. I smeared on some suntan oil, crammed a baseball cap over my head, and opened the first book, *Spanish Galleons of the Caribbean*. I flipped to the index and ran my finger down the long list of entries.

"*Estrella Matinal, Estrella Santo* . . . ah, here it is, *Estrella Vespertina.*" I turned to page 197 and began reading.

"The *Vespertina* was the smallest of the *Estrella* series. She entered into service in 1506 and began her short career with a maiden voyage that included a cargo of Spanish settlers, livestock, and the future governor of Cuba.

But unlike her sister ships, the *Vespertina* was plagued with problems from the onset. On her maiden voyage, just off the coast of Hispaniola, she encountered a tropical storm and suffered damage to the mainmast, and had to lay anchor in Santo Domingo harbor for a month for repairs.

"After that, the *Vespertina* was used to carry supplies, settlers, soldiers, and slaves between the islands of the Caribbean. She never made a return voyage to Spain, for her short career ended in 1511, due to a killer hurricane. Records show that her cargo that day included cassava plants, swine, cattle, sugarcane, five horses, seven soldiers, and an undetermined number of Indians. The Indians had been captured from an unnamed island, probably one of the Bahamas (called Lucayan by the native inhabitants) and were being taken to Hispaniola to replace the labor force there.

"Since the first arrival of the Spaniards, the Arawak (also called Taino in that region of the Caribbean) population had been rapidly diminishing due to European diseases and strenuous labor. Even though the Spaniards eventually turned to African slaves as a source for forced labor, it was easier and less expensive to raid nearby islands for new laborers.

The *Estrella Vespertina* was just one of many galleons lost to storms and other perils of the Caribbean waters. Due to the extremely deep trenches in the Caribbean Sea, most of the galleons have never been found."

I closed the book and stared across the ocean. It was mid-June and there was little chance of a hurricane, but I swear the air got cool and suddenly I shivered.

"Hey, Dusty!" I heard Jasmine's shrill voice. At the same time I looked up, a handful of water splashed over my legs.

"You . . ." I jumped up and charged at Jasmine. She squealed and dived into the pool, sleek as a porpoise. She swam underwater across the pool, then popped her head up and stuck out her tongue.

"Poor Dusty, did you get all wet?" she said in a mocking baby voice.

"If you try that again, I'll show you who's all wet," I shouted back.

"Hah, come and get me!"

I surveyed the deep pool. It wasn't very big, only about twenty-five feet long. Most of the people were sitting along a tile bench on the inside edge. Jessica was swimming laps in a steady rhythm. She was wearing eye goggles and didn't seem to notice that a couple of teenage boys were eyeballing her. When she reached one end, she somersaulted underwater effortlessly and swam back. I sighed. I would have given my big toe to be able to swim like that, with no fear.

I glared at Jasmine another minute, then brushed her away with the wave of my hand. "Ah, I'm busy. I'm right in the middle of a really good story. I'll get even with you later, when you're least expecting it."

"Party pooper, party pooper!" Jasmine chanted, but I ignored her and settled back in the lounge chair. I picked up a thick volume called *Englefeld's History of the Caribbean* and flipped to the chapter about the Arawak Indians. I began reading:

"The Caribbean Arawaks, called Tainos on most of the islands, lived an idyllic existence before the arrival of the Spaniards. Originally from South America, the Tainos developed a highly successful system of agriculture. They grew cassava in knee-high mounds called *conucos*. Around the mounds, they grew beans, squash, and sweet potatoes, which all mutually nourished each other. Because of the mild climate, the Tainos were able to harvest food year-round. With abundant starch from vegetables and protein from seafood, iguanas, and an occasional manatee, the native population grew rapidly until most of the islands were inhabited. Cassava cuttings and beans were easily transported over the ocean by canoe to start new colonies.

"Women tended the fields, working only a few hours per week. Providing fish only took the men a small part of the day. The rest of the time was spent weaving hammocks, carving canoes, making pottery, sculpting religious icons, and preparing for lavish festivals. Though no written language existed, the Tainos kept history alive by reciting long, balladlike stories called *areytos*. Children learned to sing historical ballads while they worked. Festivals included dancing and *areytos* performed by both men and women. Each village had a ball court with hoops for small rubber balls to be thrown through. The Tainos did not practice war, nor fight among themselves. Columbus and the Spaniards often remarked on their warmth, openness, gentleness, and generosity.

"With lush rain forests and tropical vegetation and few known diseases, the Caribbean truly was a paradise compared to the disease- and crime-infested European nations. The Taino Arawaks had only one enemy, the fierce

Caribs of the Lesser Antilles islands, who were their distant kinfolk but whose aggressive, warlike behavior and cannibalism sent terror into the hearts of the peaceful, gentle Tainos.

"The arrival of Christopher Columbus in 1492 began the annihilation of the Caribbean Arawaks. The Spaniards wasted no time in forcing the peaceful natives to work on plantations, raising strange new crops like sugarcane that provided no nourishment. They also spent grueling days and nights working in gold mines on the mountainous islands. These gentle people were not used to hard labor and died quickly under the harsh conditions of the *encomienda* system.

"As if that were not enough, the Spanish animals brought aboard the ships unwittingly devastated the islands. Pigs reproduced so rapidly that herds of them destroyed entire islands. They ate food crops and trampled vegetation, turning lush paradise islands into plantless mud wallows.

"But most destructive of all were the European diseases. Smallpox and measles were particularly deadly, wiping out at least one-third of the population within ten years. New diseases were also transported from Africa after the introduction of black slaves in 1509.

Malaria and yellow fever flourished due to the abundant mosquitoes that served as hosts to the parasites. These fevers destroyed both the Arawaks and Spaniards, who had no natural immunity.

"When Columbus arrived in the Caribbean in 1492, the estimated population of the entire Arawak nation was between four and eight million people. By 1500, only half remained; by 1530, the population had dwindled to only ten thousand people. In less than fifty years, the native Caribbean peoples and cultures had vanished forever. Only a few tough Caribs managed to survive on the southernmost islands near South America."

I studied the pictures of domestic scenes—men carving canoes from tree trunks, weaving hammocks, fishing with nets, or spearing manatees, and women cooking and stringing seashells. I laid the open book across my chest and closed my eyes. The cool ocean breeze and the occasional cry of a seagull soothed me like a lullaby. I could almost smell the islands as they were back then—fragrant flowers, palms, rain forest trees, and lush ferns. I could almost hear the women singing as they tended the cassava plants. They would be wearing nothing but skirts made of leaves and grass, with seashells around their brown necks and flowers in their hair. What a beautiful life it must have been before the arrival of Europeans.

Suddenly water splashed over my legs and face. I jumped and the book slid onto the deck. Girlish laughter rippled through the pool. When I looked up I saw Jasmine had two new friends. One was an olive-skinned brunette, the other a cute redhead with freckles on her nose. Even Jessica had finished her laps and was leaning on the edge of the pool, giggling. And *that* was something she didn't do very often.

"I'm warning you," I called out as I picked up the book and wiped the water off of it with my beach towel. "You're going to pay if you ruin these books. They're rare antiques that belong to the captain."

The brunette's eyes popped open, but Jessica shook her head.

"Don't believe him. He lies about everything."

I felt the blood boiling in my veins and would have walked over and smacked her, except that my parents sat in chairs near the pool and I didn't want to get into another argument with my dad. Not to mention that one of the teenage boys eyeing Jessica had muscles like a miniature Arnold Schwarzenegger, and I sure didn't want to get into an argument with him. So I picked up the book called *Treasure Hunting in the Caribbean* and flipped to the index. My heart almost skipped a beat when I saw the words *Estrella Vespertina* leaping up at me.

I had to read aloud to drown out the insults and jeers being thrown at me by Jasmine and Jessica and the two new girls.

" 'The salvage of the *Estrella Vespertina* started out to be a feather in the cap of Acme Salvage Company,' " I read. " 'Unlike most treasure hunt expeditions, which take months and even years of advance planning, the Acme Salvage Company stumbled upon the *Vespertina* while looking for another, completely unrelated galleon.' "

"Hey, bookworm, come on in the water," Jessica shouted.

"Yeah, bookworm, get your nose out of that book," Jasmine added.

"Do worms even know how to swim?" the redhead asked. They all broke out in cackles like a bunch of witches.

I muttered under my breath and read even louder and faster.

" 'Acme crew leader, Charles Noble, was astonished when his diver told him there was something resting on a shelf directly below their vessel. It appeared to be an old Spanish galleon, but it was obvious that it was not the one they were looking for. The first item the crew salvaged was a brass handle from the captain's door, extremely ornate for the times, and probably personally put there at the request of Captain Antonio Hernando Sanchez, who was known for his ruthlessness with the native inhabitants and likewise for his fine taste in metal sculptures. Sanchez went down with the *Vespertina* in 1511, when she wrecked off the Bahama Islands in a hurricane.

" 'Charles Noble was ecstatic at the surprise discovery, but this expedition was plagued with bad luck from the beginning. The diver who found the brass door handle died from an infectious cut later that week, and another crew member died when his air line got tangled in the boat's propeller. And Noble, who himself admitted that the salvage operation seemed cursed, died mysteriously a week later when—' "

"Bookworm!" The shrill notes of four girls shouting in unison made me jump out of my skin. I looked up and saw them standing above me, dripping big puddles onto the deck. They all shook their heads, spraying me and the book with seawater. Then, like the cowards they were, all four girls ran for the pool and dived in.

"That does it!" I shouted. I didn't care how much I hated swimming, or how big that boy's biceps were, I was not going to stand by and let those girls get away with their harassment. I casually walked to the pool, whistling a tune that I knew my stepsisters hated. They screeched and covered their ears, but I kept whistling and walking around the pool very calmly until I was at the far end, near the slide. I carefully stepped down onto the tile seat. From the corner of my eye, I saw my parents watching. Dad smiled at Vanessa and poked her in the ribs. She looked at me and smiled and nodded as if to say, "Attaboy, you've finally come to your senses."

The minute my toes touched the cool water, I felt something tighten up inside my stomach. But I told myself that I could do it. I slowly lowered my body down and sat on the tile seat. I pretended I was having fun, splashing water on my arms as I adjusted to the coolness against my legs and lower torso. This wasn't so bad. I hadn't panicked yet. There was nothing to worry about. I would just hold on to the seat as I swam around the edge. I would splash some water on the girls and get out. Everyone would be happy and maybe they wouldn't bug me for a while.

But that's not what happened. No, not at all. First, all four girls jumped me. Jasmine climbed on my shoulders, and the two new girls each grabbed an arm, and Jessica somehow had my left foot. I tried to hold on to the tile seat, but the girls wouldn't let me. Instead they pried my fingers loose one at a time.

Suddenly the bottom dropped from under my feet and I felt myself being pushed down. Jasmine was on my shoulders, and the other girls had my hands so that I couldn't swim. I tried, really tried to be calm and just swim, but it was impossible. My heart began pumping so fast and loud that I couldn't hear a word anyone said, just the pounding throb in my eardrums. My lungs gasped for air, but all I got was a mouthful of water.

I kicked and flailed, and felt the girls being flung in all directions. I tried to get back to the tile seat, but I got all turned around and ended up in the middle of the pool in deep water. As I sank to the bottom and water gushed over my head, I opened my eyes. Above me, I saw legs and arms of people swimming and playing. I told myself to be calm, to just swim back to the surface. I knew how to swim, for Pete's sake. But my arms and legs wouldn't cooperate. Something was pulling me down. Icy cold fingers had my legs and wouldn't let me kick. And then all the air was gone from my lungs.

I felt pressure and pain in my lungs until I knew they would burst. No matter how I tried, I couldn't get back up to the surface. Then the light faded and faded. It was getting darker, and the people's legs began to disappear. Then everything went black.

"Dusty! Dusty!"

A shrill voice woke me up, and suddenly I was gagging on water that trickled from my mouth. I gasped for air. It felt fresh and sweet and I couldn't get enough of it at first, but after several gasps I began to breathe normally again.

"Dusty!" Jasmine was shaking my arm and her face was streaked with tears. The two new girls looked pale and worried as they hovered over me. Then I saw Jessica, her face all serious as she pushed on my chest, forcing the rest of the water from my lungs.

My dad and Vanessa pushed through the little crowd gathered above me.

"That's enough, honey," Vanessa said as

she pulled Jessica off. "Let him breathe on his own now. You did good."

"Jessica pulled Dusty out and gave him CPR," Jasmine announced proudly.

"I know," Vanessa replied softly. "We saw everything."

I moaned. This couldn't be happening. Of all the people on this ship, why had it been Jessica who saved me? Why not the lifeguard, or some old woman, or even the teenage hulk?

"Are you all right, son?" Dad asked as he helped me sit up.

I tried to say "Sure," but it was a cough that came out. I cleared my throat and nodded. "Sure," I repeated. "What's all the fuss about? I wasn't really drowning. I was just teaching those girls a lesson."

"Hah!" Jessica snorted. "I suppose that water coming out of your lungs was make-believe?"

I climbed to my feet, shrugging. "Sure, it was. I had it in my mouth all along, you dummy. I sure had you guys fooled, didn't I?"

My dad's face turned from pale, to pink, to purple.

"Russell, stop it! Just stop it!"

"What?"

"Go to your room and get into some dry clothes. We'll be eating lunch in half an hour."

"And you girls don't stay in the pool too much longer," Vanessa added. "We'll be arriving at Cozumel right after lunch. I want you to be rested up so we can tour the island."

I grabbed the books and headed back to my stateroom as fast as I could, not giving my dad another chance to get on my case. I changed into dry clothes and then flung myself onto the bed.

I should have never gotten in that swimming pool. Why did I think that it would be different this time? Didn't the water always win? Now more than ever Dad thinks I'm a coward. And that stupid story about faking it? Stupid, stupid, stupid! I slammed my fist into the pillow again and again until I had made a deep pocket in it.

Suddenly I heard a noise. Clear as a bell. It was the same girl crying again. I sat up, sniffed, and ran my hand across my runny nose. I strained my ears. There was no doubt in my mind, it *was* coming from Cabin 102.

I slipped out of my room and stood in front of the heavy Spanish door with the ornate brass handle. The sobs were louder now, more pitiful and sad than last night. I tapped lightly.

"Excuse me," I said in my most pleasant voice. "Excuse me, little girl. Are you all right? Do you need help?" The crying stopped instantly. My heart pounded as I waited for her to speak or to open the door. But it was as quiet as midnight.

I tapped again. "Little girl, come to the door. I promise I won't hurt you. I'm in the cabin next to yours. I just want to know if you're okay." The silence was almost too much to bear.

I knocked again, this time not so softly.

"Listen, little girl, if you're in trouble come to the door. Don't worry, I promise not to tell anyone. I just want to make sure you're all right. If you're lost, I'll help you find your mother."

The minutes ticked away and still no one spoke or opened the door or cried. I heard voices down the hall and saw my stepsisters and parents coming. I quickly bent over and pretended to pick up something from the floor.

All the while my family changed for lunch, I lingered outside Cabin 102, but not another sound came from it. Why would a child stop crying as soon as someone came to the door? If she was alone and scared, surely she would welcome another person, especially another young person.

Why, why didn't she come to the door? I scoured my brain for answers and suddenly it hit me with a jolt. Kidnappers! If she was being kidnapped, maybe the kidnappers had her tied up and she couldn't come to the door. Maybe the kidnappers had a gun at her head, telling her to be quiet.

A sudden sense of urgency flooded over my body. As soon as we had eaten lunch, I was going to find Lionel and have him open that fancy door again. If there was a girl in Cabin 102, whether she was a stowaway or a kidnap victim or lost, I was going to turn that room upside down until I found her.

Tahni

LUNCHTIME was pretty unpleasant. Vanessa insisted we dine in the Panama Room, a romantic place filled with palm trees and tropical flowers and ceiling fans. The only problem was that we got there late and ended up sharing a table with a group of single women traveling together. All of them were schoolteachers. They spoke perfect grammar and knew everything and made me feel like I was answering questions at the blackboard.

Everyone kept sneaking glances at me, even though no one mentioned the incident at the pool. It was weird the way they just pretended it hadn't happened. The women and Vanessa talked about the ship's first port of call, Cozumel Island. Even my dad got caught up in the fever, and I must admit, I was looking forward to having my feet on solid ground for a while.

After lunch I ran into Lionel delivering a fruit basket.

"Good afternoon, young Dusty. How has your day been so far?"

"Don't ask," I muttered. "Say, Lionel, do you remember when we were in Cabin 102 yesterday?"

"Yes," he said slowly, and the smile on his lips faded.

"Well, I saw a stack of old history books in there. I love history. Do you think I could borrow some of them?"

"The ship's library has some history books."

"Those? I already read them. Our public library back home had those. I would really, really like to read some of those books I saw in Cabin 102. Could you unlock it, just for a minute, and let me grab a couple of them? I'm going crazy without anything to read."

Lionel sighed in resignation, sort of like when you tell the cashier at a hamburger joint that you didn't order onions and he knows you did, but he has to take it back anyway because the customer is always right.

"As you wish," Lionel said, fishing out his key ring as we walked down the hallway.

As I stepped into Cabin 102, once again a blast of musty cold air sent shivers up my spine. But this time I didn't care. My eyes made a quick search of the room. Nothing. No girl, no spot where she might have been tied up, no human smells, no evidence that anyone had stayed here for the past thirty years. But there were a few dark corners that needed closer examination.

"I think I see a book over there," I said, hurrying to a big, overstuffed chair and glancing behind it. Nothing. Then I looked in the closet, behind a mattress, over a stack of boxes.

"Young Dusty, the books are over there," Lionel reminded me, pointing to an old trunk.

"Oh, yeah." I sat on the trunk and picked up a book. While I idly flipped through the pages, my eyes searched every nook and cranny of that room. There really was no place left, unless there was a secret chamber someplace.

"*Uh-um.*" Lionel cleared his throat. I looked up and saw his tall frame rocking impatiently as he twiddled his thumbs.

I reluctantly got up, grabbing an armful of

books without even reading their titles. If I could somehow keep Lionel from locking the door, I could slip in the next time I heard the girl crying and catch her or her kidnappers off guard.

"Wait a minute," I shouted just as Lionel was pulling the door closed. "Could you hand me that book over there? The skinny black one. I'd get it myself, but my hands are full."

Lionel cocked his head to one side and eyeballed me like I had grown feathers or something, but he didn't say a word as he obediently retrieved the skinny black book. While his back was turned, I quickly pushed the lock button on the inside of the doorjamb.

"Thanks," I said as he put it on top of the stack in my arms. "Man, I love history books."

"*Hmmph,*" he grunted and walked away.

I just had time to dump the books on my bed, then grab my sunglasses and cap, before the ship's whistle blasted, signifying its arrival at Cozumel Island, off the coast of the Yucatán Peninsula of Mexico.

I found my parents and stepsisters already on Promenade Deck, leaning over the rail and waving at strangers on the shore. A mariachi band played lively music and the smell of Mexican food drifted out of a restaurant. Vanessa had on a huge straw hat for shade, and both of the girls had empty canvas bags just waiting to be filled with souvenirs. Dad wore his usual khaki shorts and an embarrassingly bright pink shirt with yellow-and-blue parrots all over it. He held a handful of brochures.

"Do you want to do the local Mayan ruins this afternoon, or shopping, or snorkeling, or what?" he asked.

"Mayan ruins!" I shouted. No way did I want to get in the water again, and shopping was boring.

"Shopping!" Vanessa said at the same time.

"Snorkeling!" the girls said in unison.

My dad scratched the thin spot on the crown of his head. He looked at all the eager faces in front of him, then he put his arm around my shoulders and pulled me aside.

"I want to go to the Mayan ruins, too, son. But let the womenfolk go ahead and shop today. Let them get it out of their systems, and then you and I will have all day tomorrow to do the ruins. We'll go to the big ones at Tulum, not these little ones here on the island. I promise."

"Okay," I said, trying not to appear too eager. I hadn't done anything alone with my dad since he had gotten remarried. I might even tell him about Cabin 102 and get his opinion on what to do. Yeah, a day together with my dad, minus the blond bunch, would suit me just fine and dandy.

We took a ferry to San Miguel, the main city on the island. My dad and I reluctantly followed the women from one shop to another. All the merchandise looked the same—brightly striped blankets and serapes and shawls of every color in the rainbow, straw hats, carved wooden donkeys, artificial flowers, seashells and coral, woven baskets, pottery, replicas of Mayan gods, and silver jewelry. But the women insisted on stopping in every single shop on every single street or boulevard. My legs ached, and the sun was relentless. My dad bought a straw hat to keep from getting sunburned through the thin spot of hair on top of his head. I drank a gallon of soft drinks, avoiding the local water, and sweated most of it away.

By the end of the day the women and my dad were loaded down with baskets and bags of stuff.

"You won't have any room for souvenirs from the rest of the islands," my dad grumbled, and for once I agreed with him. My whole body was aching, especially my legs and feet. I didn't have a dry spot on my sweat-drenched body by the time we climbed up the gangway and took the elevator down to our deck. The only good thing about the whole experience was that we didn't go snorkeling. And if Dad and I toured Mayan ruins tomorrow like he promised, maybe I wouldn't have to get in the water at all.

With that happy thought in mind, I took a quick shower, changed into my pajamas, and crashed onto my bed. I fell asleep before my head hit the pillow. When I woke up it was dark, and I heard the sound of muffled voices outside my room. I opened the door and saw my parents and stepsisters all nicely dressed up.

"Well, sleepyhead. Are you ready to go to dinner?"

I rubbed my eyes. "What time is it?"

"Almost seven. Aren't you hungry?" Vanessa asked. "I'm famished. Shopping always does that to me."

I groaned. "Please, don't mention shopping. I'm too tired to eat right now. I'm going back to bed."

"You'll miss the Mexican buffet," Dad said. "You know you love Mexican food."

"You'll miss the floor show tonight," Vanessa added. "It's supposed to be really exotic."

"They're going to act out a Mayan sacrifice and cut out a heart," Jasmine piped up.

"Oh, please," Jessica moaned. "That's disgusting. Maybe I'll stay here, too."

"But Brandon's going to be there," Jasmine said with a giggle and a toothless grin. "I heard him say he was going to sit next to you."

Jessica's face turned pink, and my parents smiled.

The floor show did sound tempting, but this was the perfect opportunity to sneak back into Cabin 102 and investigate. "Go on without me. I'm really beat. I'll just eat some fruit. Besides, there's a midnight buffet if I get really hungry."

Vanessa gave me that pitiful look, but my dad just pushed up his glasses and said, "Okay. You do look tired. Get plenty of rest because climbing up those Mayan pyramids will take a lot of strength."

That was unusual for Dad to agree with me, but I wasn't going to question why.

After they left, I sat on my bed eating an orange and a banana. I decided it would be best to wait until the girl started crying again so I could catch her or her kidnappers off guard. To pass the time, I thumbed through the books I had grabbed from the cabin earlier. Two of them had water damage, making the pages all wrinkled and stuck together. Another one was an oversize coffee table book with a lot of beautiful color pictures of the islands. I picked up a book called *Lost Innocence: The Demise of the Caribbean Arawak People* and started reading. The information was the same as in the history books I had already read, only with more details. The book described the fishing methods of the islanders and gave a detailed history of their nation, from prehistoric times in South America, moving to the Caribbean islands, and through settlement and expansion.

I pried apart two pages that were stuck together and smoothed them with my hand. A colored picture spread before my eyes. It was a photograph of a painting by a famous Spanish artist who had visited the islands in 1500. The picture depicted a Taino village. The people were doing their daily business. Women were combing their hair, cooking, stringing shells, tending cassava plants. Some men were fishing in a blue lagoon; others were lying in hammocks, and some were in carved canoes. Little children ran about, laughing and playing with rubber balls on the ball court. The people wore nothing but a type of leaf skirt or loin-cloth. Some wore necklaces of beads and shells.

"Your life was so peaceful," I whispered. "Why did you have to die? Why?" My finger traced the outline of the chief, a tall, handsome man with feathers in his hair. My heart felt heavy, and suddenly I wished I had never picked up this book. I snapped it shut and rolled over. The alarm clock ticked and ticked. It was nine o'clock. The floor show was in full swing. I thought I could hear drums beating and the shouts of actors portraying Mayan priests. I was really getting impatient. It was just my luck that the one night I had plotted and planned to help the girl was the one night she didn't cry.

A sudden thought jolted me out of the bed. Maybe it was too late. Suppose she had gone ashore at Cozumel. No matter whether she was a stowaway or a kidnap victim, it was only logical that she had left.

A wave of deep loneliness swept over me. I plopped back down. All day long I had been thinking about that girl, waiting for the moment that I would hear her and come to her rescue. Now I felt like a complete fool. I rolled over on my side and stared at the wall to avoid Captain Ahab's mocking stare.

I don't know what time it was when I woke up. The lights had gone out in my room again, even though I knew I hadn't flipped the switch. The stars outside the porthole hadn't moved, so I figured I must have just dozed off. I could still hear the sound of floor show music drifting down from Tropicana Deck. I heard something else, too. Crying!

I sat up, rubbed my eyes, and strained my ears. Then I heard it again, the sobbing, the pitiful crying. I should have felt sorry for her, but my heart suddenly jumped for joy. It was like the time I found my lost puppy. He had a broken leg. I should have felt sad, but I was so glad to find him that nothing else mattered.

I leaped out of bed and stumbled across the room in the darkness. On an impulse, I grabbed an apple from the fruit basket, in case the girl was hungry. I eased out of my room and tiptoed to Cabin 102. For a minute I stood there, my heart jumping like a handful of grasshoppers. I thought about knocking first, but that would give the kidnapper a warning. Suddenly it occurred to me that what I was doing was dangerous. A kidnapper might have a gun or a knife. I glanced around the hall for something I could use as a weapon, but I had nothing, not even my bedroom slippers. All I had was the apple. Well, I was a pretty good baseball pitcher, so I figured I could at least get in one good hit, grab the girl, and run.

It was now or never. I took a deep breath, and with trembling fingers seized the brass handle and pushed the door open. I flipped on the light switch.

"Hold your hands up!" I shouted. "You're under arrest!"

I found myself staring not at the face of a sleazy kidnapper but into the dark eyes and beautiful face of a girl about my age. Her lips, full and pouty, separated in surprise as she stared at me. She wore a skimpy skirt made of leaves and a crown of tropical flowers. A necklace of seashells and feathers covered her flat chest, and small painted designs adorned her brown arms. Her shiny black hair was cut in a funny style that looked like a short page-boy with bangs, but one long handful of hair fell freely down her back. She wasn't tied up, nor was there any sign of another person in the room. I felt my face turning red. She wasn't a kidnap victim any more than I was. She didn't even look like a stowaway. And that costume! It was something else.

"You're one of the floor show girls, aren't you?" I asked in a stunned voice.

She stepped back until she bumped against the big overstuffed chair.

"¿Habla español?" I asked, in case she lived on the Yucatán Peninsula. But I must admit I didn't know what I would do if she replied. That was about the only phrase I knew in Spanish.

The girl cocked her head to one side. "¿Español?" she repeated in the softest, sweetest voice I had ever heard, then shook her head.

"No, then how about French? Are you from one of the French Caribbean islands? Uh, parlez-vous français?" I used up my entire knowledge of the French language.

"Français?" she repeated, and shook her head, never taking her dark eyes off of me. Man, I had never seen such beautiful eyes. And let me tell you, her face was something special, too. Oval shaped with skin as smooth as a rose petal. She was really a knockout, but I wished she had on a few more clothes.

"My name is Dusty," I said, and held out my hand. She glanced at it for a long time, then gently, like a frightened deer or something, reached out her own hand. It was icy cold. I felt a shiver run through my body.

"Say, you must be freezing. It's so cold in here. Lionel says the air conditioner is all messed up. Why don't you take my pajama top." I slid off my polka-dotted cotton top and handed it to her. She looked at it as if it were something from a horror museum. I stepped closer to put it on her shoulders, but she stepped aside and excitedly began rattling off words in a foreign language.

"Okay, okay," I said, gently laying the pajama top on the big chair. I scratched my head. Her language didn't sound like anything I had ever heard. But from the way she was dressed, I figured she was a member of one of the South American Indian tribes, one of those that lived deep in the jungle along the Amazon. Maybe she had run away to a big city like Rio de Janeiro and ended up in the floor show. Maybe she was having regrets now and missed her village and wished she could go back home. I wished that I could communicate with her.

I smiled and held out the apple. "You can have this, in case you get hungry in the middle of the night."

The girl stared at the apple. She didn't take it, but at least her eyes didn't look so frightened now. She smiled slightly, and I knew she was beginning to trust me. I could see the tension slowly creeping from her face.

"What's your name?" I asked.

Her eyebrows twisted into a question and her dark eyes registered a big blank.

"I'm Dusty," I said. "Dusty." I thumped my chest and repeated my name, then pointed to her. A light of recognition flashed in her eyes.

"*Tahni*," she said, pointing at herself. "*Tahni*."

"*Tahni*," I whispered the name and it felt like a song on my tongue. "Hey, that's a beautiful name."

"*Dustee*," she said, pressing a cold, slender finger into my chest. She plucked a lovely white flower from the garland resting on her head and pushed it into my thick brown hair. She stepped back to admire her work, then broke into giggles.

I could imagine what I looked like with a flower in my hair, but I didn't want to scare her off, so I bowed or did something stupid like that. I knew I should give her a gift, too. I sifted through my pajama pants pockets, but all I found was a cheap red rubber ball from Jasmine's game of jacks. I bounced it on the floor once, then handed it to Tahni.

"Batey!" she squealed, then bounced it off her head, her elbow, her shoulder, then her knee. I had seen teenage boys practice for months and not come close to being that skillful and graceful.

"Hey, you're good," I said in admiration. Tahni flashed a big smile and bubbled with glee.

What a smile! I felt a jolt as if I'd been struck by lightning. But it wasn't just because of her white teeth and two perfect dimples. It was the way she smiled with her whole body—her dark eyes, her lips, her cheeks, her clapping hands and dancing feet.

I thought things were going very well, and I was about to ask her where she came from, when, without warning, she jerked her head around and stared at the porthole. She seemed to be listening to something. I strained, but I didn't hear anything, not even music from the floor show anymore.

"What's wrong?"

Tahni streaked across the room, avoiding obstacles like a gazelle. I never saw anyone move so fast and gracefully. She pointed to the porthole. I noticed that it was wide open and I could hear the slight swish of the water against the ship's hull and the soft flap of the signal flags.

"*Hurakan!*" she whispered anxiously, her face clouded with panic.

"What?"

"*Hurakan!*" she repeated, more loudly.

"*Hurakan* . . . where have I heard that word before?" I scratched my head, then suddenly remembered reading that word in one of the history books. *Hurakan* was the Taino Indian word for "great wind." It was the name of their god who brought wind and rain, and the word from which Spaniards and Americans got the word *hurricane*.

"*Hurakan!*" she repeated, and stomped her foot, impatient at my ignorance.

I ran to the porthole and looked out. The sky was black as velvet in the west, filled with millions of twinkling stars. In the east, a partial moon was casting its silvery beams on the calm dark water.

"There's no storm out there," I said. "It's really peaceful."

I turned around. She was gone. I searched the room, casually peeking behind the sofa, under the dresser, in the closet, trying not to scare her. But the only sign of life I spied was a nest of mice inside the stuffing of the big chair.

"Okay," I said to the air. "Look, I know you don't understand what I'm saying, but I'm just next door. Don't worry, I won't tell anyone you're in here. I guess you've got your reasons for hiding. I don't blame you for not wanting to be aboard this ship. I don't like it, either. I think me and you are alike, aren't we? Well, your secret is safe with me." I waited, but only silence filled the air.

"Okay, Tahni, I'm going now. I'll leave this apple in case you get hungry for a midnight snack. I know you don't act cold, but I'm leaving you my pajama top anyway. I'll bring you a shirt and pants tomorrow morning. You're going to catch pneumonia dressed like that." Still silence.

"Well, okay, then. Good night, Tahni. Remember, I'm next door." I backed out of the room, closing the door gently. I stood for a minute in front of the door, thinking about the girl, wondering where her hiding spot was.

I was still standing there when I heard voices. I looked down the hall and saw my parents and stepsisters coming.

"Dusty!" Vanessa cried out. "What are

you doing out in the hall half-dressed? Where is your pajama top?"

I glanced down at my bare chest. "Uh . . . I . . . it was that dern water faucet again. It sprayed water all over me. I was on my way to find Lionel and remind him to get it fixed."

My dad screwed up his eyebrows. "It's past eleven o'clock. Lionel wouldn't be up at this hour."

"Oh, is it that late? I must have fallen asleep. I thought it was about eight o'clock. Oh, well, I'll talk to him in the morning. Good night."

Back in my cabin, I dived under the sheets. I pretended to fall asleep while the girls bathed and brushed their teeth. When Vanessa came in to tuck them in and say good night, I heard Jasmine whisper: "I heard Dusty crying again, Mommy."

"When was that, honey?"

"I came up here to use the bathroom during the floor show. He was in the bed. I said, 'Dusty what's wrong?' but he didn't hear me."

"*Shh,* honey. Go to sleep. Dusty has some problems right now. Charlie and I are going to get him some professional help from the ship's counselor. You just be nice to Dusty and don't worry."

I heard Vanessa's soft footsteps and felt her cool hands as she tucked the sheet around my shoulders, then stroked my hair and kissed my forehead. I had to bite my lip to keep from laughing. Let them think it was me crying, I didn't care. At least then they would never suspect that it was a stowaway next door. By the time we arrived at the next port of call, I would know where Tahni had come from and what she wanted. I would help her, and maybe once in my life I would do something right.

On Top of the World

TUESDAY MORNING my family bubbled with excitement as they planned the day's activities. I wanted to slip into Cabin 102 again before breakfast, but my parents had other plans. They quickly shuffled me and my stepsisters up onto Verandah Deck for a very early breakfast. We had a perfect view of Cozumel, a sandy island set in the middle of unbelievably turquoise blue water.

After eating, passengers who had signed up for excursions boarded a ferry that looked like an oversize cabin cruiser. As it sped across the water headed for the green Yucatán Peninsula of Mexico, the waves slapped the prow and rocked the boat. That, along with the wind, made it almost impossible to walk or stand.

The blond bunch insisted on sitting outside at the front so they could feel the wind and mist in their faces. I stayed inside and closed my eyes until we had docked safely at the pier at Playa del Carmen.

While Dad and I got on a tour bus that would go south to the Mayan ruins, Vanessa and the girls, loaded down with snorkeling gear, got on another bus to take them to famous snorkeling spots. They would spend the day sunning themselves on sandy beaches and swimming with tropical fish among the coral reefs or exploring underground caverns. It sounded fun, but I couldn't wait to be alone with my dad at last.

I must admit that for a while as the bus lumbered southward, I completely forgot about Cabin 102 and my fear of water and everything bad in the world. It was just me and Dad and no blond bunch to share him with. We were going to do a male thing, climbing a Mayan temple, looking at stone steps where priests had climbed many lifetimes ago, where lives had been sacrificed, where destinies had been decided by stars and phases of the moon.

We passed through three little towns with Mayan ruins of their own, but we didn't stay long at any one, for our ultimate destination was the ruins at Tulum on the coast—and then onward to Cobá, farther inland. The way the bus skidded through turns and sped along made me wonder if we would live to see the ruins. Once we passed by some sheepherders in brightly colored serapes, shirts, and skirts. The grown-ups stared, but the kids waved and shouted as the bus driver leaned on his horn and the sheep scattered out of the way.

All of the tourists on the bus came from the cruise liner and I noticed that even a few of the nightly entertainers and three crew members had come ashore, too. They were dressed in their regular civilian clothes, having left behind their crisp white uniforms. One of them kept striking up a conversation with my dad until by the time we reached Tulum, the two men were acting like old army buddies, laughing and joking and wisecracking. The man called himself Alberto. I thought I had seen him a few times on the ship, but no matter how I strained my brain cells, I couldn't remember what he did. He could have been anything from a steward to a waiter to a first mate.

My dad bought a walking stick from a souvenir stand outside the entry gate of the ancient city of Tulum. Believe me, on the way up the steps of the main temple, El Castillo, he needed that stick. The ancient Mayans called the walled-in town City of Dawn, and I understood why as I reached the summit of the temple and looked toward the east, where the blue waters of the Caribbean gently sloshed onto the rocky beaches. To the east lay the green of the Yucatán Peninsula and the hills and jungles of interior Mexico.

At the top of the structure, carved in the same white-gray stone as the temple, the image of a god stared back. He had feathered wings and appeared to be falling or diving through the sky.

"He is the Descending God," Alberto explained. "No one knows what he stands for, perhaps the setting sun, perhaps a honeybee." Alberto knew everything. It should have been fun to have him along, I guess, but what I really wanted was to be alone with Dad so we could talk. I wanted to ask him about Tahni, without actually telling him she was hiding in Cabin 102. One of those hypothetical questions. But Alberto was with us all the time.

We messed around for another hour, then hopped back into the tour bus and headed west toward another Mayan city called Cobá, about an hour's drive away. How different this terrain looked than the open, rocky ground near the City of Dawn. The forest grew dense, and the air was filled with the sounds of insects and exotic birds. Maybe the tour guide was just joking when he mentioned jaguars and boa constrictors, but I spent a lot of time looking over my shoulder after we got off the bus and walked deeper into the jungle.

When we at last arrived at Cobá, I was amazed to see that half the structures were still buried under hundreds of years of jungle growth and appeared to be no more than big green humps. But at least one of the temples had been cleared of vegetation, and its tall, gray stone steps beckoned to us.

We climbed and climbed and climbed. Most of the tourists stayed below, sipping fresh fruit drinks and eating snacks sold by a vendor, or walked around some of the other sites. But we kept on climbing, and all the while I heard parrots and toucans below us, whistling and screeching. It reminded me of being at the zoo.

"Whoa, boy," Dad said as he leaned on his walking stick when we reached the summit. "The air up here must be thin or something."

"I counted one hundred and twenty steps," I announced between gasps.

Alberto laughed. He didn't seem to have any trouble breathing at all. "This is the best exercise in the world," he said, drawing in a deep breath. He swept his hand toward the jungles and a sparkling blue lake. "It is home of the gods—the most beautiful place on earth."

I wasn't going to argue with him. The view was amazing. It's funny how sitting on top of a high place sort of removes you from all your problems. It's like the problems are down there crawling around like hungry wolves trying to find you. But as long as you're on top of a temple or the roof of a house or in a tall tree, they can't reach you. I laughed out loud.

"What's so funny, Dusty?" Dad asked as he sat down on the top step beside me and rubbed his left knee. Alberto joined us without even being invited.

I shrugged. "Nothing."

"I think Dusty likes the solitude and majesty up here," Alberto offered. "Up here you can put your worries and troubles in perspective. And they become as small as ants. Am I right?"

I gave him a sidelong glance and shrugged again. There was something about this man that was getting on my nerves. I stood up.

"Hey, Dad, let's go explore that little flat spot over there."

"That was the altar where the priests performed sacrifices," Alberto explained.

I thought of hearts ripped out while still beating and women thrown to their deaths into deep sinkholes. I swallowed hard. "Hey, cool. Let's go check it out, Dad."

But my dad waved his hand at me. "You two go on. I'm bushed. I want to rest another minute. This old football knee is acting up again. Go on."

I gritted my teeth. The whole point of getting up was to get away from Alberto, not to be alone with him. But I didn't want to do anything to upset my dad. In spite of his wheezing and complaining about his leg, this was the closest we'd been in ages. It reminded me of the days when we used to do stuff together, the days before Vanessa and her pesky daughters entered the picture.

I walked to the edge of the temple. It, too, had the image of the Descending God carved in white stone. I leaned over the edge and watched a parrot hopping in the treetops below.

"Are you enjoying the cruise?" Alberto's lilting accent cut into my thoughts.

"It's okay, but I'm not much of an ocean person. I like the solid earth beneath my feet."

"Ah, but there are a lot of wonderful activities for children and teenagers on board the ship, aren't there? My own son used to enjoy the scavenger hunt most of all. His team usually won. Of course, now he is a teenager and thinks he is too old for childish games. Now he spends most of his time in his room on these voyages and doesn't seem to enjoy them at all. Why do you think he spends so much time in his room?" The dark eyes stared a hole in me. I felt like a worm on a hook and glanced toward my dad. He was still sitting down and didn't seem concerned at all that this overly nosy stranger was interrogating his son.

"Maybe he's just bored with it all," I said with a shrug. "Well, I'd better get back and see if Dad is all right."

"Just a moment more, please. It isn't often that I get to talk to another boy about my son. Now, let's suppose that my son is bored, as you say. Then what do you suggest that I do to get him to join the others his age? How can I persuade him to join his mother and me and his two sisters?"

My eyebrows shot up. This guy was really getting on my nerves. I glanced at my dad again and caught him looking at me from the corner of his eye. When he saw me, he turned around real quick. An alarm started going off in my head.

"You say your son is on the ship? He lives with you?"

"No, but since I divorced his mother, he takes cruises with me often."

"You're divorced?" A second alarm started ringing in my head.

Alberto nodded. "And I recently remarried. A wonderful woman with two lovely daughters. But my son seems resentful and distant. Why do you think he acts that way?"

My face began to get hot. By now the alarms were sounding so loud I couldn't hear the birds and insects and other tourists talking below. I wanted to turn around and run down the 120 steps. I wanted to push Alberto over the edge and watch him splatter below. Or better still, watch him take part in a Mayan human sacrifice; see his heart cut out by a priest decked out in feathers and masks.

"Dusty? You didn't answer my question."

"You know, Alberto, you never told me exactly what it is that you do on the ship, did you?"

He cleared his throat and shifted his weight. "Why, I—I assist the ship's doctor. I am a type of physician." He smiled and his perfect teeth seemed unbelievably white against his tanned skin.

Yeah, right, you mean you're a headshrink, I thought.

"You know, it just occurred to me what might be wrong with your son," I said. "I think I know what you can do."

"Yes?" The dark eyes lit up and he leaned closer. I swear, he rubbed his hands together like a praying mantis before it devours its prey.

"Well, the way I see it, your son is being pressured too much to fit in and be like everyone else. Just leave him alone."

Alberto put his hand to his chin and nodded wisely.

"And, of course," I said, staring him straight in the eyes, "the *worst* possible thing you could do to him is to send him to the ship's psychiatrist. That would really make him mad."

I watched the color rise to Alberto's cheeks.

"Touché, Dusty," he said, and gave a little bow. "I'll tell your father what you said."

"Don't bother. I'll tell him myself," I said, and shoved passed Alberto. I don't know what got hold of me, maybe it was Mayan spirits, but I had the uncontrollable urge to tell my father just what I thought.

As I stomped across the ancient stones, I rehearsed in my mind what I would say and do. I would square my shoulders, look my dad right in the eyes.

"Dad," I would say, "you blew it. You ruined our day together by dragging this lousy headshrink along. He's been giving me the fifth degree since we left the bus. I had plans for us. I wanted to tell you about this girl I met in Cabin 102 and get some advice. I was even thinking of telling you how much I hate water and maybe even telling you it was me that caused your and Mom's divorce. But how can I tell you now, knowing you think I'm crazy?"

I stopped behind my father. He was still sitting down. It would be so easy to kick him, to shove him down the steps. I looked at his dark hair, the same color and curliness as my own. He used to carry me piggyback when I was little and pretend he was a horse. I could close my eyes and still hear the funny neighing noises he used to make and see the way his glasses would always fall off. We were friends back then. He didn't think I was weird or in need of a psychiatrist. Why did things have to change?

I guess I made a little noise in my throat, because Dad suddenly turned around.

"Oh, Dusty, I didn't know you were there," he said, pushing his glasses up on his nose. "How was the view?"

I clenched my fists and tried to swallow down the sharp lump choking my words.

"Dusty?" He stood. "How was the view?"

"Boring," I said with a shrug, then ran back down the 120 steps. I shot past a statue of the Descending God. What was it Alberto had said? "Nobody knows what he stands for." Well, I truly identified with that god. Nobody knew what I stood for, either.

Funny, the climb up hadn't seemed so difficult, but the lower I descended, the more depressed I got. By the time I reached the bottom, tears were blurring my vision. I stumbled over a bump in the ground and almost fell on my face. Without even waiting for my dad or Alberto, I trotted down the white road made out of stones sunk in the ground centuries ago.

I arrived back at the tour bus before anyone else, except for the driver, who squatted on the ground, smoking a cigarette. But I didn't care. I sat in the last seat next to the window, fighting back my tears. The dense trees and the darkness and the extreme heat choked the air until I thought I was going to suffocate. Sweat beaded up on my forehead and trickled down my temples.

I closed my eyes and tried to think of something cool. The first thing that popped into my head was Tahni's cold brown hands. I imagined them touching my face. Then I imagined her terrific smile, and the funny way she stomped her foot when she was angry, and the way she giggled when she put the flower in my hair. I thought about her strange accent and sweet voice. I know this sounds crazy, but I swear all of a sudden she was in the seat next to me. I could smell the flowers in her hair and feel the coldness that always surrounded her. That was impossible, of course. But all the same, I began to cool down, and I didn't dare open my eyes for fear that she wouldn't be there.

"Tahni," I whispered to the air, "why did Dad do that to me? Why does he think I'm crazy? Just because I don't want to play silly games with my stepsisters or get in the swimming pool. And why can't I just tell him

I'm afraid of water and be done with it?" I sighed.

I thought I heard Tahni's contagious giggle, and though I knew it couldn't be, I giggled myself. I heard her sweet voice singing and I sang along with her to pass the time. About half an hour later, I heard voices coming down the trail.

"Thanks, Tahni," I said to the air, and opened my eyes wide. Just as I expected, Tahni was not there and the bus was silent, save for the wind swishing through the open windows. By the time the tourists climbed on the bus, moaning and groaning about their aching legs and feet and mopping their sweaty brows, I felt as cool as a cucumber and a big smile was on my lips.

I noticed right away that my dad was not talking to Alberto. They sat about as far apart as they could. Alberto sat in the front next to a good-looking teenage girl, while Dad limped to the back of the bus and plopped into the seat right in front of me, groaning as he adjusted his long legs.

He wiped the sweat from his forehead with a very, very damp handkerchief, then twisted around in his seat.

"Dusty . . ." He paused as if struggling for

the words. "I guess it wasn't such a bright idea to bring Alberto along like that without telling you who he was, but I, I . . . just don't know what to do," he stammered.

I shrugged and kept looking out the window.

"Maybe you don't like Alberto, but what he says makes sense. You need to talk to someone about what's bothering you. I wish it could be me, but—"

"I'm okay, Dad, really," I interrupted and turned to face him. "Everything's cool." I don't think I fooled him, but I guess he was too tired to argue and I could tell his knee was hurting something awful. He closed his eyes and slept for the rest of the trip back to Playa del Carmen, where we boarded the return ferry.

Frankly, I was glad to get back aboard the *Historia* that afternoon and practically leaped for joy when the departing whistle shattered the air.

The blond bunch skipped aboard, cheeks more tanned than ever and bubbling with stories about coral reefs and colorful fish that practically ate from their hands and dolphins that romped beside them. All in all, I'd say they'd had a better day than Dad and I.

I was dead tired, and I knew I should take

a nap. But my dad was right about one thing, I needed to talk to someone. As weird as it sounds, considering she couldn't even speak English, I knew the person I needed to see was Tahni.

Child of the Sea

AS THE SUN set over the jungles of the Yucatán Peninsula, the *Historia* slowly pulled away from Cozumel and headed east. She would push ahead all night and all the next day, arriving at the next port of call, the Cayman Islands, in the wee hours of Thursday morning while everyone slept. I dreaded the Cayman Islands, with the powdery white beaches and famous coral reefs that had earned them a reputation as a scuba diver's paradise. I was running out of excuses for not snorkeling or swimming in the ocean.

My family was exhausted from the day's events and decided to take a nap before dinner. It looked like everyone aboard had the same idea, because when we arrived for the late seating, the main dining room was packed.

That evening's entertainment was an extravagant musical revue. While my dad ogled showgirls in skimpy dresses and Vanessa drooled over the male dancers, I sneaked back to my stateroom. I snitched a flower-covered blouse and pair of pink stretch pants from Jessica's dresser drawer. I grabbed another apple from the fruit basket and a complimentary chocolate mint from the bed.

Luckily, Lionel had not discovered the unlocked door to Cabin 102. The heavy oak door opened with a creak. As usual, the cold air slapped me in the face and sent chill bumps racing up my arms and legs.

"Tahni," I whispered as I flipped on the lights. "I brought you some clothes and food." I saw right away that my pajama top was exactly where I had left it. Tahni must have had a hot nature to be able to stand the cold room. But I noticed that the apple had been half-eaten. At least she wasn't starving. I called for her again and again. Nothing.

Except for the apple, there was no evidence that she had been there. I searched the corners and under things and behind things, but I knew it was useless. She would not come out until she was ready. I saw some more Caribbean history books behind the old dusty trunk. I sat down on the floor and was flipping though one of the books when I heard a voice behind me.

"Hurakan!" the voice said excitedly.

I jerked my head around and saw Tahni standing under the opened porthole and pointing toward the sea. I swear the porthole had been closed when I entered the room, and I had not heard her open it. She was as sneaky as a cat.

"Hi!" I said. "Where did you come from?" I smiled, but she only repeated her phrase over and over.

"Hurakan! Hurakan!" she whispered. She even grabbed my hand and forced me to look out the porthole.

Just as I expected, the sky was clear and the water was smooth as glass. "There's no storm out there," I said in my softest, kindest voice. "Come over here and sit down, Tahni. I brought you some clothes and another apple. If you'd rather have oranges or bananas or mangoes, I can get some of them, too." I held out the apple.

She took it, turning it around in her slender, brown hands. I showed her the clothes. She looked very confused, so I pulled the pink stretch pants on over my shorts and slipped the flowery blouse on over my tee shirt. I did a silly little dance and acted like a girl. Tahni giggled and took my hands and we sort of skipped in a circle for a minute, dodging some boxes. I was out of breath, but she didn't seem to be breathing at all. As a matter of fact, she was singing!

"Tahni, if only I could find out where you're from and why you're here." I sighed and sat down on the old trunk, then scooted aside some of the books to make a place for her to sit. As I removed Jessica's clothes, an idea suddenly pounced upon my brain. I grabbed one of the books, the one that had the most maps and pictures. I flipped to the page covered with a map of the Caribbean Sea.

"Where is your home?" I asked, pointing to the map.

Tahni's dark eyes scrutinized the page, and her brown fingers touched the paper delicately. She muttered words of her language, but there was no hint of recognition in her eyes. I heaved a sigh. She heard me and looked up. Her eyes glistened with sadness and she touched my face softly. She sighed, too, and spoke a few more words.

"Who are you?" I asked again, and stood

up. The book fell to the floor and opened to a reproduction of a painting of a Taino village. I didn't even bother to pick the book up but began pacing and kicking stuff out of my way. How could I communicate with this girl? How could I find out who she was and why she was hiding in this room? I paced to and fro, dodging chairs and coffee tables, mumbling to myself. Then I heard a little yelp and wheeled around.

Tahni was kneeling on the floor over the book, her fingers gently touching the picture. She was speaking rapidly, excitedly.

"*Bohio,*" she said, and looked up at me. She pointed to the picture. "*Bohio.*"

I leaned over and picked up the book. The caption beneath the picture read, "Taino women tend cassava plants grown in mounds called *conucos,* while the men weave hammocks outside their houses, called *bohios. Bohio* could also mean home. Haiti was often called Bohio, because of the creation story that claimed the mountains of Haiti as the birthplace of their race."

Before I could say another word, Tahni pointed to the cassava plants, each growing in its own small cone-shaped mound of dirt.

"*Casavi,*" she said. Then she ran her fingers across the mound of dirt. "*Conuco,*" she said.

"*Bohio, casavi, conuco,*" I said softly. "You know how to speak Arawak?"

"*Bohio, casavi, conuco,*" she repeated, her voice bubbling with excitement. Tears of joy twinkled in her eyes. She pointed to every single thing in the picture, telling me the words in her language.

"*Canoa,*" she said, pointing to the twenty-foot-long canoe being carved and burnt out by several men. "*Tabaco,*" she said, pointing to a cigar. "*Barbacao,*" she said, this time pointing to a stick framework over which some meat was being cooked by a fire. "*Batata*" was her word for sweet potatoes.

"*Ah, hamaca,*" she giggled, pointing to a long white hammock stretched between two poles inside an open-ended hut covered with palm thatch. "*Caçique.*" This time her fingers touched a man dressed in fine regalia, with exotic bird feathers radiating out of his hair like a peacock's tail and seashells and coral necklaces and copper bells hanging from his neck.

Caiman was a crocodile; *iwana* was an iguana; *caney* was a big, fancy hut; *nagua* was a white cotton skirt that some of the women wore; *dujo* was a chair shaped like an animal; *guagua* was a baby; *batey* was a game played with a rubber ball. On she chattered. Trees, flowers, fish, lagoon, sea, birds, man, woman, girl, boy—she had a word for everything in the picture. I found a pencil stub and some blank envelopes on the dresser and scribbled down as many of the words as I could, guessing at the spelling. I flipped through the book, looking for other pictures, and each time I found a new one, Tahni laughed, reminding me of a dolphin frolicking in the ocean.

One picture showed villagers dressed festively, dancing around a bonfire.

"*Areyto,*" Tahni cried out. She leaped up and danced around, her feet beating out steps to a drum that pounded only in her head. She began reciting what sounded like a ballad and made me pound the hollow trunk every few seconds to keep time with her singsong voice. The story went on and on until I finally had to make her sit down again. We continued looking at pictures and she settled down for a while as she told me strange new words.

But when Tahni saw the picture of a girl diving for pearls, she leaped up again and made swimming motions with her hands and pretended to gather oysters in a basket. It was more fun than watching a movie, and with each new scene I learned more about her.

Obviously Tahni lived on one of the islands in the Caribbean. She lived in a small village and loved to dive for pearls, and she loved to swim in the water of a peaceful blue lagoon near the village. Her father was important, probably the chief of the village. No wonder she acted so impatient with me; she was probably used to getting her way and being treated like royalty.

When I had finished going through every book in the stack with Tahni, she crumpled to the floor, put her hands over her face, and cried. It was the same sad, pitiful sobbing I had heard before. I put my arm around her cold shoulders and tried to comfort her. I made faces, and put on the flowery blouse again, and stood on my head. She stopped crying and sniffed. But just as I was getting her to smile, she suddenly turned her head toward the porthole.

"*Hurakan!*" she gasped, then jumped to her feet.

"Oh, no, not again," I mumbled as she streaked to the porthole.

"*Hurakan! Hurakan!*" she said, her voice filled with panic.

My heart pumped faster, and though I knew it was pointless, I rushed to the porthole and looked out. As usual, the sky was clear and the moon had already risen. The ocean was calm and empty, except for a few little fishing boats and a big yacht with white sails.

"There is no hurricane, Tahni. It's clear as a bell out there," I said. When I turned back around, she was gone. "Shoot!" I said, and kicked the floor. "She did it again."

I looked everywhere but couldn't find her. She was a genius when it came to hiding. I knew it was pointless to look anymore, so I hung the clothes on the back of a chair. I placed the fresh apple on the trunk and took the half-eaten one with me. I stepped out of the room and gently closed the door behind me.

"Dusty!" I heard familiar voices call my name.

I gulped and spun around. "Jasmine? Jessica? What are you doing out here?"

"Looking for you," Jessica said. "What were you doing in there?"

My brain raced. "Uh, uh, getting something to read. It's a storage room full of junk and old books."

"I wanna see," Jasmine pleaded.

Against my better judgment, I opened the

door, ran in, and grabbed the oldest, most musty book in the stack, then rushed back out.

"See? Just old history books."

Jessica crossed her arms and glared at me but didn't say anything.

"Please, don't tell my dad," I said. "Let's keep it a secret."

"Ooh, I love secrets," Jasmine said, dancing a little jig and clapping her hands. "Is it okay, Jessica? Can we have a secret from Mom and Charlie?"

"Please, Jessica?" I pleaded.

"What's it worth?"

I was afraid she would say that and was ready.

"I'll buy you a nice souvenir at the next port."

"Something expensive. No junk," she said, then grabbed Jasmine's hand and dragged her down the hall.

I leaned against the door and let out a long sigh of relief. It didn't last long because before I could get inside my cabin, Lionel walked by carrying a small, antique trash can that must have come from the Chinese clipper cabin (it had golden dragons entwined along its sides). An unpleasant reek drifted out of it.

"*Hmm,*" he said, eyeballing the apple in

my hand. The eaten parts had turned brown and looked pretty disgusting by now. "I suppose you're finished with that?" Lionel held up the trash container and I dropped the apple in. It hit with a loud metallic plunk.

I smiled. "Thanks, Lionel."

Lionel stared at the apple, then picked it up and turned it over. "*Hmm,* where did you get this?"

Panic coursed through my heart. "Uh . . . why do you ask?"

"I'd say that by the looks of these teeth marks, a hungry little rodent has a full tummy now."

"A rodent? You mean like a mouse? Yeah, I guess a mouse ate it. I found it under the dresser. One of the girls must have dropped it there. Mice, yeah, I think I did hear the pitter-patter of tiny feet last night." I was pleased with Lionel's idea. I couldn't have thought up a better story myself.

Lionel looked up, an expression of annoyance on his face.

"And I know exactly where those mice are coming from," he said, not trying to hide the disgust in his voice. "I saw a nest of them in the stuffing of a chair in Cabin 102."

"Cabin 102?" Suddenly my story didn't

sound so great. I had to keep Lionel out of that room. "I didn't notice any mice when we were in there the other day."

Lionel must not have even heard me. He pursed his lips and a look of determination filled his eyes. "I guess I'll have to put out some rat poison this evening. Exterminating those vile creatures is unpleasant work, that's for sure, but it has to be done."

I swallowed hard and felt like someone had punched me in the stomach. If the poison bait would kill mice, what would it do to a frightened stowaway girl named Tahni?

A Midnight Swim

I LEARNED a really big lesson that night: never, never tell your sisters a secret. The next day, Wednesday, was pure misery for me. Every time I saw Jasmine or Jessica talking to my parents or a steward, my nerves got all frazzled. I imagined that they were spilling the beans. Even worse than that, those sweet-faced girls had devious minds and used my secret like the threat of nuclear war. We were at sea all day, so I became their main distraction.

"Dusty," Jasmine said in her innocent little voice when she caught me crossing the deck on my way to the gift shop, "the horse races are about to begin. Hurry, let's go!"

"What are you talking about? You can't have horse races on a ship."

"Oh, they're not real horses. It's a game. People act like horses and someone rolls dice and the horse has to move that many steps. The spectators place bets on them. Come on, Dusty, be my horse."

"Oh, brother," I muttered. "No, thanks, Jasmine. I don't feel like a horse today. A slug, maybe, but not a horse."

Then she crossed her arms and pouted her lips. Her big baby blue eyes took on the look of a man-eating shark's hungry black eyes. She tapped her toes. "Why are you so mean, Dusty? I'm not mean to you. I'm keeping your dumb old secret about that cabin next door. You haven't played one game with me since this cruise started. You're so mean."

Now, she didn't come out and say, "Hey, buster, if you don't play horsey with me, I'm going to blab your secret," but I got the message. So guess who got to be a horse?

Both Jasmine and Jessica nearly died of hysterics while I nearly died of humiliation. Vanessa had talked Dad into being a horse, too, and it became a close contest between me and him. I won, but there was no glory in the victory. I felt stupid all over.

After that I thought my brotherly duties

were over for the day, but I was so wrong. They had just begun. Jessica, using the same logic and insinuating ever so slyly that she might reveal my secret, talked me into one of those stupid scavenger hunts just before lunch. She needed me to serve as a buffer between her and Brandon the hunk. His brains must have been stored in his big toe. He was fourteen and I was only twelve, but he couldn't figure out the clues. They were so lame that my team won without much effort.

That is how my day went, with me playing one game after another—more like a slave than a brother. And every time Vanessa and Dad happened to see me, they smiled and nodded and said, "Good! Wonderful! Great! That's the spirit!" until I wanted to puke. I even saw Dad talking to Alberto once and imagined that their conversation went something like this:

"Morning, Alberto, have you noticed the change in my son, Dusty?"

"Ah, yes, Señor, it is no doubt because of my sensitive and shrewd approach to the problem. After our intellectual dialogue on top of Cobá temple, he no doubt finally saw the errors of his ways. Yes, thanks to me you can expect him to join his stepsisters and

participate in the ship's activities for the rest of the voyage and grow up to be president of the United States."

That afternoon I ducked behind a lifeboat and slipped away from my stepsisters' grasp long enough to buy a small blank notebook from the gift shop so I could write down all the Arawak words that Tahni had taught me. I saw Lionel briefly and found out that he had not put out the rat poison yet because he was too busy and wouldn't have a chance to get to it until very late. That would give me enough time to warn Tahni later that night while everyone else was asleep.

I wanted to go to my room to write in the notebook, but I never made it there. The girls pounced on me and insisted I go to an ice-cream party; then it was help them make an arts and crafts project for a contest; then a Coke party; then a game of Ping-Pong. They wanted me to join them in the pool for a swim just before dinner. Now, this is where I wanted to draw the line, but that secret hovered in the air above my head like a granite boulder getting ready to drop if I did the slightest thing to upset the darling stepsisters.

So I sat on the edge of the shallow pool and dangled my feet while Jasmine splashed around with some little kid she had taken a liking to. I tossed them a beach ball until my arm was sore, but at least I didn't have to get in the pool.

After dinner the blond-haired fiends forced me to sit through a magic show. Man, I hate magic shows—the men in the black tuxedos and top hats, the disappearing rabbits, and the doves flying around the room. All I could think about was Tahni and about that poison that Lionel was going to put out.

While everyone gasped and clapped for the magician, I wrote in my notebook. I don't think my parents even noticed, because they were at the other end of the row. I think they were in shock to see me there.

I divided the notebook into sections with headings labeled plants, animals, people, and things. After transcribing every Arawak word from the back of the envelopes I had used as scratch paper, I discovered that I could make a crude type of sentence like: *chief cassava hammock*. Which, of course, means *"The chief was eating cassava while he lounged in the hammock."* There was an obvious lack of verbs in my notebook, but I would work on that the next time I saw Tahni.

After the show, on the way back to our

stateroom, my dad wrapped his arm around my shoulders.

"Well, that was some show, huh, Dusty?"

I forced a smile. "Sure, Dad. It was great."

Vanessa laughed. "See, honey, you can have a lot more fun doing things with family. This is a lot better than being cooped up in your room with an old, stuffy book, now, isn't it?"

I started to protest, but then the image of Tahni sitting in that cold room, waiting for her one and only friend to visit, made me nod my head like a robot.

"Yeah, it was great fun. Let's do it again real soon."

I said good night and got into bed in record time. I didn't want the girls to have any excuses for staying up late.

"Turn off the lights," I said to them. "We have to get up early in the morning. We'll be in the Cayman Islands by the time we wake up. You'll want to be ready for all that shopping and snorkeling."

Thank goodness they agreed, and soon the room grew quiet except for the slow, steady breathing of the girls and the funny little creaks and groans of the ship as we plowed through the night.

I got dressed in the dark, then slid the notebook and pencil into my shirt pocket. I also grabbed three history books that I had taken from Cabin 102 earlier. I turned the brass handle on the heavy oak door and let out a tremendous sigh of relief when it turned. Obviously Lionel had not been in tonight with the rat poison.

"Tahni," I whispered. "Tahni, it's me, Dusty. Where are you?"

I surveyed the room carefully, every cobwebbed corner and pile of junk. Everything was as I had left it—books on the floor, clothes on the chair, apple on the trunk. Once again the apple was partially eaten. I was examining it when I heard something scurrying across the floor and saw a flash of dark gray vanish beneath the overstuffed chair. Then I heard a squeal and saw Tahni jump up from behind the chair.

"Tahni!" I said, laughing.

She ran out to the middle of the room, pointing to the mouse and clucking her tongue, and complaining in her native language. When she turned, she acted as if she had just noticed me.

"*Dustee!*" she cried. A smile lit her face and she clapped her hands, then threw her arms around my neck. She plucked another one of the flowers from the garland on her head and stuck it in my hair. She patted my cheeks, all the while speaking in that soft voice that was as sweet as music.

Taking my hand, she plopped down on the floor next to the books and pulled me down beside her. She pointed to the big book with all the colorful pictures.

"Okay, okay," I said, and opened it up. Once again she pored over the pictures, tracing her slender brown fingers over the people, the plants, the ocean, the village huts. I took out the notebook and recorded some new words. I even managed to get her to tell me some verbs by acting them out. I pretended to walk, run, swim, swing in a hammock, sit, stand, lie down, roll over, sleep. On and on we went, until I had enough words to communicate.

I tried out one of the sentences I concocted: *"Tahni swim ocean dive pearls,"* I said in the Taino language. Tahni clapped her hands and giggled so loud I was sure she would wake up my stepsisters.

I don't know how long this went on, but once again we looked at every picture in the stack of books. Then I remembered the three other ones I had brought. We flipped through them. Some of the pictures were the same. But when we came to a picture of Taino slaves being loaded into a Spanish galleon, Tahni gasped. Her face turned pale and she shivered.

"*Español,*" she whispered, and for the first time her sweet voice sounded bitter.

"Yes," I said in disbelief, "that's right. That's a Spanish galleon. How do you know that, Tahni? Did you study about Spaniards in school?"

Even though we had communicated a few simple sentences—about swimming in the ocean or eating cassava or weaving a hammock—I had not been able to get Tahni to tell me where she lived or why she was on this cruise liner. It had never occurred to me that she might have gone to school and studied history like other kids.

Tahni's eyes grew darker as she stared at the picture. She leaped to her feet so fast that I dropped the book. She stomped on the picture and spat over one shoulder. "*Español!*" she said between clenched teeth.

"Geez," I muttered. "I get the picture, Tahni. You don't care for Spaniards very much. I guess I can't blame you; they really mistreated your ancestors. But shoot, that was almost five hundred years ago. Talk about holding a grudge."

Tahni's cloudy face didn't clear, and her lips pouted. I tried to soothe her, but with no luck. She stomped her bare feet on the book over and over. Angry words spewed from her lips. I heard the words for *mother, father, sister, brothers,* and I thought I even heard the word for *hurricane,* but she was talking too fast for me to keep up. Then without warning she crumpled to the floor and covered her face with her hands. The sobbing started, worse than I had ever heard it before.

"Tahni, don't cry. Please, don't cry." I put my arms around her cold shoulders, but she didn't stop. Her sadness surrounded me like icy arms. I knew that if I didn't get away, I would be crying, too.

"Tahni, let's look at some happy pictures. Come on. Let's talk some more. *Tahni swim ocean dive pearls.*" I repeated the silly little Taino sentence that had made her laugh so much earlier. She sniffed, and I thought I heard a little chuckle, but it was mixed in with the sobs.

I grabbed one of the books and flipped to the picture she loved so much, the one of children playing in a quiet lagoon and men diving for pearls. The water was so blue and beautiful. It was the same aquamarine color as the water in the swimming pool up on Lido Deck.

"That's it!" I said, jumping up. I pulled Tahni to her feet. "Come on, Tahni, I know how to make you feel better." I glanced at my wristwatch. It was past one o'clock in the morning. I should have been in bed. I would be dead tired tomorrow, and all the shopping and touring of the Caymans would wear me out. But I couldn't leave Tahni like this. I opened the door, glanced up and down the hall, then pulled her out the door. Her dark eyes opened wide, and she dragged her feet.

"Don't be afraid," I whispered. She seemed to understand, for she became as light as air and followed me without protest.

We took the stairs to avoid making noise on the squeaky elevator. I opened the door to Lido Deck and walked outside. The air felt moist and warm compared to Cabin 102. The stars that usually filled the sky like a billion twinkling diamonds had been drowned out by the light of a full moon that flooded the deck in silver.

The moonlight danced on the aquamarine water of the deep pool, making it look like a handful of iridescent pearls. Tahni's tears had dried by now. She didn't seem to notice anything on the deck, no lounge chairs, no tables or umbrellas, no shuffleboards or life preservers. Her eyes stared straight ahead at the shimmering blue water of the deeper pool.

I pulled the safety net back, put there each night to keep nosy kids like me out of the water. Tahni poised, then dived in, leaving her flower crown floating on the surface. Like a graceful dolphin, she skimmed smoothly, flawlessly underwater until she reached the other end. She popped her head up, shook the beads of water from her hair, and laughed. Then she dove again, straight to the bottom. She picked up something shiny. When she popped up again, she was next to me. Her face beamed with joy as she handed me a new copper penny.

She dove again and again, retrieving little things lost by passengers—a hairpin, a child's bracelet, a nickel. All the while she swam, so graceful, so at ease, I felt envy creeping through my bones. Why couldn't I love the water like she did? To her the water was a friend, to me it was an enemy.

After Tahni had retrieved every scrap on

the bottom of the pool, she stopped in front of me. I sat on the ledge, my bare feet dangling in the water. She tugged at my feet, playfully tickling them. Then she grabbed my hand. Her magical smile beckoned me. I started to make up some excuse, then it occurred to me that it was pointless to lie to Tahni. She didn't understand English. No wild fabrication would rescue me this time. If I refused to go in, she would take it to mean that I didn't like her. It would spoil her fun, her wonderful happy mood.

I removed my shirt, then took a deep breath and slowly slid down the side of the pool onto the tile bench. As usual the panic, the dread, the tight knot in my stomach and the feeling of paralysis in my legs took over. I forced a smile.

"The water's nice," I lied.

Tahni laughed and pinched my leg, then swam in front of me as playful as a sea otter. She kept her eyes wide open and a smile on her face, even under the salty seawater. I managed to splash some water on her and to swim a few feet by holding on to the tile bench. I relaxed a little. As long as I wasn't in the deep water, I would be all right.

After twenty minutes or so, I had

completely forgotten about where I was and who I was. Tahni and I chased each other along the edge of the pool. We laughed and splashed and I was actually having fun. I was no longer Dusty, Fearer of Water, in a cruise liner swimming pool. I was now Dustee, Taino-Arawak boy, Lover of Water, and in the middle of a peaceful blue lagoon on some unnamed Caribbean island.

Only when she grabbed my hand and started swimming out into the middle of the pool did I resist. I put on the brakes and broke free, barely making it back to the ledge. She turned and looked at me with a big question in her dark eyes.

"Dustee swim," she said in her language.

"No," I said. "Dusty . . . *Dustee sleep.*" I put my head on my hands and closed my eyes.

Tahni shook her head as if to say, "What a wimp," and dived again.

I crawled back onto the seat and watched her. She was beautiful, and if I used my imagination, she was diving for pearls instead of bobby pins.

The sound of footsteps made me turn around. I climbed out of the pool, ran across the deck, and looked around the corner of the little snack bar. Lionel was walking in my direction and he didn't look too happy. I ran back to the pool to warn Tahni, but she was gone.

"Young Dusty! What on earth are you doing in the pool at this hour? I heard you all the way from my quarters." Lionel stood with his hands on his narrow hips, wearing a deep red velvet robe over striped silk pajamas and red house slippers. "Did you remove the safety net?"

"I'm sorry, Lionel. I just wanted to practice some dives. I'm too embarrassed to do it during the day. You know how it is."

"*Hmm.*" Lionel's sleepy eyes and unshaven face didn't show too much sympathy. "That safety net is there for a reason, young man."

"I'm really sorry, Lionel. It won't happen again," I said as I helped him roll the net back over the pool. After he left, I put my shirt back on and looked for Tahni, but once again that girl had managed to vanish without a trace. Even her flowers were gone.

Back on Calypso Deck, I shivered with dread at the thought of stepping inside her cold cabin. And with my wet skin and pants, I nearly froze on the spot when I entered. I knew

Tahni must be freezing, too, but she had not touched the clothes I left her.

"Tahni, Tahni," I called over and over, but she didn't come out. I was not even sure that she had returned to the room.

As I stood there shivering, it occurred to me that I had completely forgotten to tell her about the mice and the poison. But there was no way I could warn her now. She couldn't read any note I might leave. There was only one solution: I would have to invent a really good story to keep Lionel from putting the poison out.

I waited for Tahni as long as I could stand it, but finally I couldn't take the coldness another minute. I was shivering and my teeth were chattering, so I returned to my room.

As I changed into dry clothes and crawled into my roll-away bed, I wondered if maybe taking Tahni to the swimming pool had been a mistake. Instead of making her happy, maybe it had only reminded her of her home. But where was Tahni's home, her *bohio?* As I closed my eyes and fell into an exhausted sleep, I knew that my next task would be to find the answer.

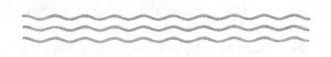

The Best Laid Plans
of Mice and Men

THE NEXT MORNING, Thursday, the breath-taking white beaches of Grand Cayman Island twinkled outside the porthole. My parents and stepsisters had already dressed and gone topside for breakfast. I only vaguely remembered them trying to wake me up at seven A.M.

As I lay in bed eating a banana and mango from the complimentary fruit basket, I mulled over my stockpile of excuses for getting out of swimming and snorkeling today. There were no Mayan ruins to visit, just coral reefs and beaches and water sports everywhere. It was indeed a water-lover's paradise and a water-hater's nightmare.

I sat up and ran my fingers through my hair. Maybe I could fake some tropical disease. How about malaria or yellow fever? Parasites would be good. I was wondering which one to choose when I heard keys jingling, then the sound of the door to Cabin 102 opening.

I bolted out of bed and ran to my door. I saw Lionel standing in the hallway, a red-and-yellow box in his hand.

"Yo, Lionel!" I exclaimed, making him jump out of his skin.

"Young Dusty! Are you attempting to give me a heart attack?"

"Sorry, old pal," I said, slapping his back. "Whatcha got there?"

"Rat poison for those despicable rodents."

Panic seized my body. I had to think fast and shake the cobwebs out of my excuse machine. I had fallen asleep last night before coming up with a really good one. I took a deep breath, crossed my fingers, then plunged in.

"Oh, you don't have to do that," I said with a smile, and gently closed the door to Cabin 102. "I already took care of the mouse in our cabin. I set up a little homemade trap last night. I put a little piece of cheese on a ruler and balanced it over the wastebasket. When the little critter stepped out on the ruler to get the cheese, he fell—*kerplunk*—right into the can. I tossed him overboard last night."

"*Hmm.* That's a highly unorthodox way to trap mice." Lionel eyed me with those black eyes, and I really didn't think that he believed me for a minute. "Nevertheless," he finally said, "where there's one mouse, there is another. I'm sure I saw their nest in Cabin 102." He opened the door again. I jumped in front of him and blocked the entrance.

"No!" I said, then laughed nervously. "You shouldn't put out rat poison."

"Now, see here." Lionel shot me an unsympathetic glance. "It's my duty to remove unwanted rodents. Why, pray tell, shouldn't I put out this poison?"

"Hey, dead mice will stink up the place, right?"

"I will remove the deceased bodies. I've done this before. Filthy mice on board are inexcusable." He tried to step by me, but I leaned on the door frame.

I ran my fingers through my hair, groping for another believable excuse.

"Look," I finally said, lowering my voice. "It's . . . it's my little sister, Jasmine. You know, the cute little blond girl. Well, she has a thing about killing animals. When she heard that you were going to kill the mice next door, she went into fits and cried and cried. That's why I fixed up that deathless mousetrap. That's the way we do it all the time at our house."

"You have mice in your house?"

"Oh, sure, lots of them. Jasmine thinks of them as her pets. She loves mice. We catch spiders and flies, too. She hates to see anything die. Why don't you put that rat poison away, at least until this voyage is over. I'll set another deathless trap tonight to catch the other one, if you want me to."

Lionel sighed. "Well, I would hate to upset that sweet little girl."

"Yeah, right," I muttered, then grinned. Once again the great never-failing excuse machine had come to the rescue. "Thanks, Lionel. I really appreciate that." I slapped his back affectionately.

"*Hmmph,*" he snorted, then closed the door. I felt a wave of relief surge over me and let out a long, slow breath. All of a sudden I felt carefree and in the greatest mood. I followed Lionel as he walked down the hall a few paces, stopping with him at a linen closet. He wasn't in a very good humor, by the way he shoved those towels and soaps around. I tried to think of something to get his mind off dead mice.

"By the way, Lionel," I said in my most cheerful voice. "Do you mind if I ask you a history question about Jamaica?"

"Why certainly not; I pride myself in knowing the history of my country."

"Do you know anything about the Indians that lived in the Caribbean? Specifically, the Taino branch of the Arawaks."

"Quite a bit. What is your question?"

"The books I've been reading said they all died from disease and hard labor and starvation after the Spaniards arrived."

"Sadly, that's true."

"Did any of them survive? Is it possible that there is a small Taino village someplace on one of the Caribbean islands? In America, we have reservations where Native American tribes live much like their ancestors did and speak their own languages. Is there anything like that in the Caribbean?"

Lionel rubbed his chin.

"*Hmm.* There are still some Carib Indians in the Lesser Antilles. And I do recall reading that there was a tribe that claimed to be pure Taino. I think it was located in Cuba. But that was fifty years ago, when I was a schoolboy in

Jamaica. Some experts claimed that the tribe was fake, but I don't know what finally happened. Why do you ask?"

I shrugged. "Oh, no reason. I like history, that's all."

"I have a good book about Taino culture in my quarters. You're welcome to read it."

"Thanks, that would be great."

"But you'll have to get it very soon. I'm leaving the ship after the stop in Jamaica."

"What do you mean, you're leaving the ship?"

"Remember, I told you this is my last voyage."

"But I thought you were at least going back to Miami."

Lionel shook his gray head. "No, when the *Historia* sets sail from Jamaica Friday night, I will be sitting on the porch of my little house, sipping rum from a coconut shell. Thirty years of service on one ship is long enough, don't you agree?"

"Yes, but this cruise won't be any fun without you. I have a million questions to ask about Jamaica and the *Queen Mary* and stuff like that. You're the only friend I have on board."

A smile slid across Lionel's lips. "I'm deeply touched, young Dusty."

"I was hoping you could show me some of the sights on Jamaica. Like that sugar plantation where you were born."

"I should think it rather boring for a young man."

"You don't know what boring is until you've been sightseeing with the blond bunch." I formed praying hands and put them under my chin. "Please, please say yes."

"Well, my service with the *Historia* officially ends Friday morning. I am free to leave anytime after that. All I need to do is pack my clothes and a few mementos, but those will fit into one duffel bag. Sad, isn't it, that thirty years of a man's loyal service fits into one duffel bag." His face looked even longer than usual as he heaved a sigh.

"Ah, but think of all the wonderful things you can do now, Lionel. Fishing and swimming and seashell-collecting, dancing and singing and drinking rum all day. Why, de island is paradise, mon." I slipped into a fake Jamaican accent.

Lionel leaned his head back and roared with laughter.

"Very jolly. I should listen to you more often, young Dusty."

"Does that mean we have a deal?" I held out my hand.

"We have an appointment indeed." Lionel squeezed my hand. "Shall we say Friday at one P.M.? And be prompt. I do not tolerate tardiness."

"Aye, aye, sir." I saluted. About that same time I saw my family strolling down the hall, full from a lavish breakfast, chattering about the day's plans.

"Hi, Lionel," Jasmine piped, flashing her toothless grin. "Whatcha got in that box, chocolate mints for our pillows?"

The blood drained from my face and I gagged. Quickly I made a signal to Lionel, but it was too late.

"That's rat poison, silly," Jessica said calmly as she slid past us and unlocked the door to our stateroom. "He's probably trying to kill that disgusting mouse I saw last night."

"Oh, dear, do we have mice?" Vanessa asked, glancing down at the floor nervously.

"Mice!" Jasmine shrieked. "In our cabin? I hate mice! Oh, they make me sick." She made the most awful face I've ever seen and hid behind Vanessa. "Mommy, I hate mice." She began to whine pathetically.

"I see," Lionel said slowly as he turned to face me. "Did you hear that, young Dusty? The sweet little child hates mice."

I tried to grin, but my lips were frozen. Even my casual shrug didn't function right. "Well, hey, maybe I was wrong."

Lionel ignored me. He leaned over and patted Jasmine's head gently. "Don't you worry, young lady, I'll get rid of those nasty mice. I'll put down rat poison this very moment." Before I could make a move, he marched to Cabin 102, opened the door, and walked inside.

"No, you can't put out poison. Lionel, please, don't," I begged.

"Russell, let the man do his job," my dad added as he unlocked his cabin door. "You know how Jasmine feels about mice."

"But rat poison is dangerous. Somebody could get killed."

"What are you talking about?" My dad scrunched up his eyebrows. "That just looks like an empty storage room to me. Who might get killed?"

"Well, a stowaway for example. She might be hiding in there."

"Really, Dusty," Vanessa said with a shake of her head. "That's very unlikely, I'm sure. Mice carry diseases. Let Lionel exterminate them."

Lionel gave a little bow. "Thank you, ma'am."

My heart pounded as I watched Lionel place a piece of cheese on a tray in the middle of the floor. As he opened the box of poison, I felt tears rise to my eyes. I could see Tahni cheerfully nibbling at the cheese, thinking it was a gift from her new friend, Dustee. Pain would rip through her body, she would convulse, then collapse cold and lifeless to the floor, like a dead rat.

"No!" I shrieked, jerking the box from Lionel's hand. "I can't let you kill her!" I ran to the porthole, opened it, and threw the poison overboard. The box floated a few seconds, then sank beneath the blue water. At least for a little while, Tahni would be safe.

"Oh dear," Vanessa said, putting her hand over her mouth.

"Russell! What is going on? Have you finally snapped?" My dad marched across the room and grabbed my arm.

"You've got to believe me. There *is* a stowaway in here. If you put out poisoned food, she might eat it and die." My heart was thumping like a dog's tail and I hated myself for betraying Tahni's secret, but I had to protect her. Expressions of disbelief flashed across all the faces around me.

"Calm down," my father said. "What makes you think there is someone in that cabin?"

"I saw her."

My parents turned to Lionel. "Have you seen anyone, Lionel? Or any evidence of a stowaway?"

Lionel shook his long, narrow head slowly.

"No, sir. I searched the room thoroughly a few days ago looking for a teapot."

"Tell him about the apple, Lionel. She ate half of it. You saw it."

"Is that true, Lionel?"

Lionel shifted his weight uncomfortably and cleared his throat before speaking. "Actually, the teeth marks appeared to be those of a rodent. And I saw a nest of mice in the excelsior stuffing of a chair. Thus the rat poison."

I felt my heart sink to the bottom of my shoes, and I would have slumped to the floor if my dad had not been holding on to my arm.

"Russell," he said, trying to control his voice. "This is the final straw. You're not going to ruin our vacation with your uncontrollable lies. If I have to, I'll pack you up and fly you back home right now." He let go of my arm and I fell to the floor.

"Dusty, dear," Vanessa said as she leaned over and helped me stand back up. "Are you sure this stowaway is not just a figment of your imagination? It's not uncommon to invent playmates when you have problems that need to be solved. Jessica used to have a little make-believe friend who helped her through those first few months after her father died."

"No, Vanny," my dad interrupted. "There's nothing make-believe about throwing a box of rat poison out a porthole. There's nothing make-believe about disrupting our vacation. It's pure selfishness."

"Oh, Charlie." Vanessa sighed and her blond eyebrows crinkled up. "Let's just forget all this and go snorkeling. The brochures say the coral reefs here are the prettiest in the world. Did you know this is where Jacques Costeau did all his research in his little vessel, the *Calypso*?"

My dad shook his head and crossed his arms. "I'll not have a spoiled brat for a son."

Vanessa crossed her arms and tapped her

foot. "He's not spoiled. He just needs help. You said so yourself just two days ago."

They both started talking at the same time, their voices getting louder and louder.

I couldn't believe it was happening all over again. The accusations, the yelling. Just like with my mom and dad when I was younger. That had ended in divorce. I had never heard Vanessa and Dad argue over anything more important than how many minutes to jog on the beach. Now, because of me, they were at each other's throats and little Jasmine was whimpering.

Suddenly I couldn't stand it another minute. I put my hands over my ears and ran as fast as I could down the hall to the stairwell. I stumbled as I climbed up one step after another, blinded by the tears forming in my eyes. By the time I reached the top of the stairs, my stomach was churning and a sour taste was rising up my throat. I burst out the exit door, ran to the rail, and just made it in time to hang my head over the edge of the ship and retch into the ocean. My whole body shook with sobs. Big streams of saliva dripped from my mouth. I must have looked like a mad dog.

I heard whispers behind me and sensed

that a crowd was gathering. Then I heard soft footsteps and felt long, skinny fingers wrap around my arms and lift me to my feet.

"What's wrong with him?" someone asked.

"He has a touch of fever, that's all," I heard a familiar voice say. "Come along, young Dusty, let's get you to sickbay. A few saltine crackers and ginger ale will take care of this." Lionel led me to the elevator and down to the infirmary. The nurse smiled sweetly, stuck a thermometer in my mouth, and put me on a tiny cot covered with icy cold sheets.

I guess you have to be careful what you wish—it just might come true. I had thought about pretending to get some tropical disease, and now the nurse assured me that I did indeed have a fever. Not much of one, but just enough to warrant a couple of aspirin and a cold compress on my head.

"I'll tell your parents where you are," Lionel said.

"Tell them to go ahead and snorkel and sightsee without me. I'll be all right here."

"Not to worry. I'll take care of everything. Everything." His kind eyes glistened with something—maybe it was understanding, maybe it was compassion. But somehow I knew that I did not have to worry about him putting rat poison in Cabin 102 again.

"Thanks," I said, and closed my eyes.

By lunchtime, I was feeling fine. I ate a big chef's salad and half a chocolate pie. I went ashore and stopped at the first souvenir stand I saw. I bought Jessica a seashell-shaped pendant carved from coral, Jasmine a big stuffed manatee, and my mom a canvas tote bag with sea turtles painted on it. I used up most of my money, but I had enough left to buy a big pink conch shell. I lifted it to my ear and heard the ghostly swish of the wind and waves. I knew Tahni would love it.

And she did. Although Lionel had not said anything to me, I know he left the door to Cabin 102 unlocked on purpose. So, just after 2:00 in the morning, as the *Historia* cut through the ocean toward Jamaica, once again Tahni and I sneaked to the empty swimming pool. In the lounges, the musicians had packed up their instruments, and the last notes from the piano bar had drifted away, leaving the ship in eerie silence.

The cool night air and breeze sent shivers

up my arms. The last thing I wanted to do was swim, but Tahni took my hand and pulled me toward the pool.

"Dustee swim," she cried out.

"Well, if you're a figment of my imagination, Tahni, I sure have good taste," I said, and sighed in resignation. I didn't want to swim, but it sure would feel good to forget about my own troubles for a while.

Tahni was like a little kid with the conch shell. She held it to her lips and blew it again and again, making a low, hollow sound. I chased her around the pool, and before I knew it I had rolled back the safety net again and was in the water. We wrestled for the shell, she dropped it, and I dived for it and caught it before it hit the bottom.

It wasn't until I was on the bottom that I realized where I was. The old familiar panic started to set in and my heart began to race. But from out of nowhere, Tahni's hand came to rest on my shoulder and guided me to the edge of the pool. When I came up for air, I couldn't believe what had happened. I had actually swum in ten-foot-deep water and survived. I hugged Tahni and kissed her cheek. She giggled, then splashed water in my face and charged toward the middle of the pool again.

I followed her fearlessly—well, almost fearlessly. As long as she stayed next to me, I could do anything. But if she swam away, my legs would feel like concrete and I would start to sink. We played games—she as fast and agile as a mermaid, me more cautious and less daring. She also discovered the slide that night. I thought she would never stop climbing and sliding. She even convinced me to try it a couple of times.

After over an hour of play, I heard someone coming, and this time I knew I couldn't afford to get into trouble again, so I dashed out with Tahni. We replaced the net and ran down the stairs and back to her room. I was freezing, so I put on the pajama top that had been on the back of the chair since the first time I met her. Luckily for me, no one had noticed it earlier that day, with all the rat poison excitement. I was still cold, so I pulled Jessica's pink stretch pants over my wet swimming trunks. As usual, Tahni wanted to look at the pictures. But I was too cold. My teeth chattered and my fingers shook too much to hold the pencil to take notes. This irritated Tahni to no end, and she stamped her delicate foot and chastised me.

"I have to leave now, Tahni," I finally said,

and left her standing in the middle of the room, her dark eyes shimmering.

My conscience felt like a ton of lead that night when I heard her crying again, but I was exhausted from staying up past two o'clock for two days and from swimming with Tahni. I fell into a deep sleep and didn't wake up until Jasmine jumped on my chest.

I groaned and rolled over, but the bright light from the porthole shot into my eyes.

"Get up, Dusty. You're going to miss breakfast," Jasmine said.

"Where are we? What day is this?"

"It's Friday and we're in Jamaica, mon," Jasmine said, and began singing the old reggae song "Montego Bay" and swinging her small hips.

"Friday." I sat up and rubbed my dirty hair. Today was Lionel's last day aboard the *Historia*. And he had promised to show me around after lunch. With his knowledge of the island, maybe the two of us would be able to find a rustic Taino village that was missing a cute little girl with flowers in her hair.

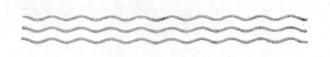

In Search
of Paradise

JESSICA WAS MUTTERING to herself as she sifted through her closet. "Where are they? I know I packed my pink pants and that blouse with flowers all over it." She swung around, her hands on her hips. "Jasmine, have you seen them?"

"Nope."

I felt my face go pale when she turned on me.

"Dusty, have you seen my pink pants?"

"Oh, yeah, right. I just slept in them last night," I said. When she wasn't looking, I slipped off the pink pants, rolled them up in a ball, and tossed them into the open closet. The look of puzzlement on her face when she found them was worth a million dollars. I had to bite my tongue to keep from laughing.

I ate a breakfast of scrambled eggs, waffles with strawberries and nuts on top, bacon strips, and fresh pineapple juice. I needed my strength for a long day of sightseeing. My dad pushed his glasses up on his nose as he shuffled through the travel brochures. Vanessa put her hand on my forehead.

"Feeling better today?" she asked.

I nodded, my mouth full of waffle. "Must have been a stomach virus."

"Maybe it was rat poison," my dad muttered as he looked at me over the rim of his glasses. But Vanessa gave him a signal with her eyes, so he looked back at the brochures.

"Here are the choices we have today," he said. "Glass-bottom boat over the coral reef, snorkeling, sailboards, parasailing, Dunn's River Falls, the botanical gardens, Green Grotto Caves, Fern Gully, and horseback riding."

The girls and I started arguing. As usual they wanted to do anything that involved water and I wanted to do anything that took place on land. Jessica wanted to go horseback riding along the beach with Brandon the hunk and wanted me to go along as her protector. No way! Finally they all agreed on the waterfalls and botanical gardens for the morning, with snorkeling, parasailing, and other water sports that afternoon. I groaned and slumped lower in my chair.

"Now what's wrong?" my dad asked.

"Lionel wants to show me some sights this afternoon. Did you know he's retiring? This is the last day I'll ever see him. He wants to show me the sugar plantation where he grew up and the old slave quarters. Can I go?"

"Oh, Dusty, why do you want to go to an old building full of stuff that belonged to dead people?" Vanessa asked. "You need to get more exercise. I haven't seen you snorkeling or swimming in the ocean one time on this vacation."

"Please, Vanessa, I'll do anything. I'll clean house for the next month, I'll take out the trash without complaining, I'll wash the dishes. Let me go with Lionel. Please."

Vanessa glanced at my dad.

"I don't know, Dusty," Dad said. "I don't think you should go off somewhere alone. You're in a strange country now. You don't know the laws. Anything could happen."

I gritted my teeth and clenched my fists. "Lionel is no stranger. He's nice. And smart. He reads more books than I do."

I must have said something right, because Dad and Vanessa exchanged glances then nodded. "Okay, son," Dad said. "You and Lionel can visit the plantation while we're at the beach. But you still have to go with us to the waterfalls and the gardens this morning."

If things had been different, I might have hugged my dad, I felt so happy. But instead I just nodded.

After breakfast we disembarked, then climbed into a small, local boat that looked like it would sink any second from the number of tourists crowded aboard. The motor spewed and sputtered as the waves slapped against the boat's sides. It even died once and took five minutes to start up again. I tell you, my stomach and my heart shared the same spot the whole trip.

We followed our guide to an area of the beach where a huge waterfall spilled right into the ocean. It was beautiful and weird at the same time. He made us join hands and warned us about slippery rocks as we started up. The women squealed and men laughed as we picked our way through the tumbling, foamy white water. The roar was deafening, and we had to shout to hear each other. The guide took our photo and told us we could buy a copy of it at a little stand set up in front of the ship when we got back.

I guess I had fun. At least it was fun watching the girls slide down the rocks and hide under little cavelike spots. The best part was when Brandon the hunk got stuck on a rock and couldn't get down.

After the waterfalls, still dressed in our swim trunks, we toured a lush tropical botanical garden. But the hot air dried us off fast. The time flew and before I knew it I was back on the ship changing into fresh clothes and gobbling down another fantastic meal.

After lunch I looked for Lionel to make sure he had not forgotten the sugar plantation. And I needed to know if he was mad at me for that rat poison incident. I found him stooped over a box of mementos in his quarters. He was humming a lively reggae tune, a sure sign that he was in a good mood. But when I said hello, he stopped singing and a frown crossed his face.

"Well, well. Did you have an entertaining swim last night? Or should I say this morning. It was past two A.M., wasn't it?"

I gulped and forced a smile. "What . . . what are you talking about?"

Lionel straightened, and there in his right hand was my pink conch shell. He placed it to his lips and blew out a mournful blast.

I ran my fingers through my hair and giggled.

"Uh, okay, I admit it. I did take a little dip. How'd you know it was me?"

"Never mind. But I must warn you, the new chief steward, Preston Willoughby, will not be so willing to look the other way. Those swimming rules are for your protection. It's not safe to be swimming alone late at night. If you slipped and hit your head, or had a sudden leg cramp, there would be no lifeguard to rescue you."

"Lionel, let's not talk about leg cramps," I said as I took the conch shell. "This is your last day aboard this old tub. We should be celebrating. How many years did you say you worked here?"

"It's been thirty years I've watched my homeland fade away from the bow of the ship, wishing I were staying. Tonight when the *Historia* pulls away, I'll be on that dock watching *her* fade away. She's been good to me, but now I'm coming home." His old eyes glistened a minute, then he shook his head and pointed to the conch. "Now, see here. You're trying to make me forget about your escapade last night." He wagged a long, bony finger. "I should report this to the captain."

"But you promised to show me the sugar plantation."

It seemed like forever before Lionel finally nodded. "So I did."

I threw my arms around his skinny old neck. "Thanks, mon," I said in my fake Jamaican accent, and shook his hand.

Lionel met me at the gangway as he promised at precisely one o'clock. I hardly recognized him. His knobby knees stuck out of bright yellow shorts and his thin arms protruded from a pink shirt covered with green parrots. A straw hat perched on his head at a cocky angle and a white grin spread across his face.

A little tour bus took us to the old sugar plantation, where we transferred to a tram being pulled by a tractor. The smell of sugarcane, pineapples, and banana blossoms filled the air all around us. The guide explained the history of the plantation and the region in general, from occupation by Arawak Indians, to the Spanish explorers, to British landowners and

African slaves. The tram stopped in front of the old slave quarters.

"I used to play here as a child," Lionel explained. "It seems like only yesterday my father was calling to me to quit hiding and 'come cut de sugar.' "

The Great House of the plantation was pretty dreary looking on the outside—really just a big square, stone building. Inside was better, with lots of fancy antique furniture. But the one thing that caught my eye was a huge painting—at least six feet across—hanging in one of the rooms. It was exactly like the picture in one of the history books, the picture that Tahni loved so much.

"Is that a Taino village?" I asked the tour guide.

"Sure, mon," he replied in a rolling Jamaican accent. "You been readin' histories o' de island?"

"Yes. I'm really fascinated with the Indians who live here. I've heard that there's a real Taino village on one of the Caribbean islands. Do you know which one?" *Please don't say Cuba,* I prayed, and kept my fingers crossed.

"Real Tainos? I'm not sure. But if you want to find out more about de Tainos and Arawaks, visit de museum a few miles from here. Nobody know 'bout it 'cause it's not in de travel brochures. She haf a lot of artifacts, and even a replica Taino village."

My heart began pounding. "Lionel, we've got to go there. Please." I know it isn't a pretty sight when a boy begs, but I was desperate. Somehow I knew that Tahni's future was tied to that village. There had to be a reason for her being dressed in leaves and flowers. I knew now that she wasn't a member of the floor show troupe. Maybe she lived in the replica village. If not, surely the curator would be able to tell me where the last remaining Taino village was.

Lionel only vaguely remembered the museum, and with great reluctance agreed to go there after a break for tea. At a little café, he ordered finger sandwiches, cookies that he called biscuits, and dark, spicy tea laced with rum. I was on needles and pins waiting for him to finish, but he was in no hurry. The island atmosphere had gotten hold of him and a lifetime of strict British discipline had been washed away in only a few hours. He walked slower and seemed more interested in smelling flowers, gossiping with strangers, and sipping rum than pursuing our destination. In his bright pink shirt and yellow pants, he fit right in with the other islanders.

The Arawak Museum was not a very famous place. It wasn't on the tour route and it wasn't on the tour map. We had to take a taxi, which did not make my wallet very happy. But the museum was free, though there was a donation box at the front door.

Disappointed is not the word to use to describe how I felt when I saw the inside of the museum. All the displays consisted of were a few artifacts like fishing spears, seashell jewelry, pieces of hammocks, and diagrams of cassava. The gift shop had the same books I had already read and a smaller reproduction of the big painting hanging in the Great House on the sugar plantation. The only book that interested me was one about the Taino-Arawak language. But I didn't have enough money to buy it.

"Where's the Taino village?" I asked the clerk behind the cash register. He had his head buried in a Stephen King novel and greatly resented me interrupting the story.

"In de bock. An' please hurry, we close at five o'clock."

I pulled Lionel away from the stack of postcards and cheap knickknacks on a table and rushed to the back. We stepped into a dark room, stale and hot. There were several glass cases with little straw huts and small figures representing Arawak Indians. The displays reminded me of something our third-grade class had done one year when studying Native Americans of the United States.

I spun around, taking in one tiny scene after another.

"This can't be it," I whispered to myself. Lionel was leaning over the glass case that depicted the first arrival of Spaniards. A tiny galleon rested in a blue bay, and tiny Arawaks greeted the strangers with garlands of flowers and baskets of cassava and seashells.

"*Hmmph*," Lionel said as he took a pair of reading glasses from his pocket and examined the scene. "Very detailed work."

"This can't be it!" I shouted so loudly that Lionel jumped.

"Young Dusty! *Shh!* I'll remind you that you are in a museum."

"Is dere a problem?" The clerk entered the room, jingling his key ring in an obvious attempt to get us to leave before closing time.

"This can't be it," I said to him. "The guy on the sugar plantation said there was a replica Taino village here."

"Yes," the man said slowly, his dark eyes rolling toward the glass cases and his dark hand giving a brisk wave in the same direction.

"But I thought the replica was real."

The man's eyebrows screwed together. "What you mean, mon? Bigger?"

"No!" I shouted. "I mean real. Real people."

"*Ah . . .*" Lionel nodded and smiled. "I think young Dusty thought there would be real people acting out life in a Taino village. Like at Williamsburg, Virginia, where residents wear costumes and pretend to live the everyday life of colonials."

"No, no, no!" I shook my head like an angry baby throwing a temper tantrum. I might have even stomped my foot. "Not actors, Lionel. Real Tainos living in a real Taino village. Like when I went to Arizona and visited a Zuni town."

Lionel looked at the clerk and a sudden light of recognition passed over both of them. They both smiled, as if to say, "*Oh, how cute and quaint and ignorant this young American child is.*"

"Young Dusty, that isn't possible. I told you there are no Taino Indians anymore."

"But I've seen one. A girl dressed in clothing just like in that painting."

"Perhaps de child was dressed for a special program at school," the clerk said, glancing at his watch and rattling his keys again. "Sorry, mon, but you really haf to leave now. I haf to close in five minutes."

"But I saw her, a real Taino, and she speaks the Arawak language fluently. She's not an actor, she's real." I ran to the gift shop and grabbed the book about the Taino-Arawak language. "See, look, here's the word for chief—*caçique;* and here's the word for home—*bohio* ... These are the words she uses. She's not an actor. She's a real Taino!"

The clerk looked at Lionel, and this time his eyes were not laughing.

"Listen, mon," the clerk said as he put his hand on my back and steered me toward the front door. "De Taino Indians be extinct. Dey be dead—every single one. Mr. Columbus and his boys, dey take care of dat five hundred year ago. De only ones who lived married block slaves and now dere skin be as block as mine. Listen, mon. You did not see a real Taino."

"Then what did I see?" I said in a voice that felt heavy and empty at the same time.

"Someone is playing a practical joke, young Dusty. Pulling your leg, as you Americans call it," Lionel offered.

"Or maybe you see a ghost, mon," the clerk said. His laughter rocked the crumbly brick walls. "Dat's it, mon. Maybe you see a Taino ghost."

Tahni's Story

I DIDN'T STOP SHAKING all the way back to the cruise ship. Lionel didn't talk much either until just before the taxi stopped at the docks.

"Young Dusty, I don't know who . . . or what . . . you've seen, but I know that you believe it's real. And that's all that matters."

"Do you believe me?"

The old eyes blinked. "I don't know. I've sailed with the *Historia* for thirty years and some very strange things have happened. Too many deaths and too many mechanical problems. But I never told any of the captains anything."

"You saw her?"

Lionel shook his head. "I never saw anyone, but my grandmother taught me to believe

that some things never die. Love, hate, re-
venge. She said some souls are taken before
their time and grow restless. I thought she
was a foolish, superstitious, uneducated old
woman. But sometimes I just don't know." He
drew in a deep breath and patted my hand. "I
wish I could finish out the rest of the cruise
with you, but you'll be on your own after tonight. I wish you well." I felt the warmth and
strength of his old hands on top of mine.
Hands that had served Clark Gable and Swedish royalty, hands that had served ordinary
people like me.

"Thanks, Lionel. You're a good friend. I'll
miss you."

"Well, I've enjoyed knowing you, too,
young Dusty. Now, it's on to face the music.
My little house is waiting for me."

"Aren't you going to the luau down at the
river tonight?"

"No, I've seen it many times. You'll enjoy
it. The fire-eater is a distant cousin of mine."

"But it won't be fun without you to explain things."

Lionel laughed softly, then tossled my hair.
"You're a fine lad, Dusty. No one's ever asked
me to show them the sights of Jamaica before.
I've always been just another servant to the

rich, the famous, and the ordinary folk of the world. I appreciate your devotion, Dusty, and I have a little memento to give you to remember me by."

He handed me a brown paper sack that had the name of the museum gift shop on it. My mouth fell open as I lifted out the tiny black book about the Taino language. I turned it over in my hands slowly.

"Lionel! This is the best present anyone's ever given me. Man, I wish I had something to give you."

Lionel shook his head and held up his hand. "Don't worry, you have given me more than you know."

I walked Lionel back to his room and helped him carry his duffel bag and one box of belongings to the waiting taxi. We shook hands and I said good-bye, fighting back tears and trying to swallow down the sharp lump in my throat.

In the lobby I ran into Jasmine and Jessica, who were beaming with stories of coral reefs, colorful fish, sailboards, and seashells. Bags of new clothes and souvenirs hung from their arms. They had bought new outfits to wear to that night's luau, so had Vanessa and my dad and nearly everyone else coming up the gangway. I must have been the only person who didn't own a shirt with flowers or parrots on it.

Disembarking for the luau would not begin until seven o'clock. That meant I had a free hour to visit Tahni and find out if she was real or a ghost.

As I waited for the elevator and then rode down to Calypso Deck, I examined the book Lionel had given me. It was small, like a little Bible, with a silky black cover. When I opened it, the musty smell of mold rushed into my nostrils.

"Whew, it smells like this book was written in the days of Columbus," I muttered. It turned out I was right. The book was written by a Catholic missionary named Friar José Madrigal. He had been assigned to save the souls of the Arawaks on one of the islands called El Jarron. The foreword to the book stated that historians were not sure where El Jarron was located, but it was probably one of the Bahaman Islands that back then was called Lucayan by the Indians. The friar's diary had been translated in the early 1930s by a British linguist and reprinted in the 1970s. Obviously it had not made the best-seller lists.

Friar Madrigal briefly discussed the lifestyles of the natives, his efforts at converting them, their rapid succumbing to diseases. But the majority of the book contained his records of learning the Taino language. The last part of the book was a long list of vocabulary words and some basic grammar rules.

"*Muchas gracias*, Friar Madrigal," I whispered, and kissed the cover of the book. I scrambled out of the elevator and hurried to Cabin 102, making sure no one saw me sneak inside the frigid room.

"Tahni," I whispered urgently. I flipped to the vocabulary list and found the Arawak words for *Come here*. I repeated the phrase three times before I heard the familiar giggle and felt Tahni's cold hands cover my eyes. I removed them and turned around.

"*Taino,*" I said, for according to Friar Madrigal, that was their greeting word. It meant "peace." It also meant "good" and "noble" and was the name used for the upper class. I squatted low and touched the ground with my hand, a sign of respect.

Tahni's eyes grew wider and she let out a little gasp of surprise.

"*Taino,*" she whispered, and likewise knelt.

I took her cold hands into mine. "Tahni,

you must tell me who you are. Where did you come from?" She squeezed my hands, then took a flower from her hair and pushed it into mine, smiling and giggling all the while.

"I can't believe you're a ghost," I said with a sigh. "I can feel your hands. I can see your smile. I can hear your laugh. You *can't* be a ghost."

I flipped through the vocabulary list searching for the right words to make a complete sentence. *"Where do you live?"* I finally asked in Taino. At this rate it was going to take the entire hour for me to ask her just a few simple questions. I would have to write down her answers as accurately as possible and translate them back in my room later that night. *"Where do you live?"* I asked again, speaking the Taino words very slowly.

Tahni's eyes lit up.

"Bogati," she said softly, and pointed to the book on the floor. It was still opened to the village scene.

"Good!" I whispered, and scribbled her reply in my notebook.

"Why are you here on this ship?" I asked. *Ship* was a hard word because the Taino language did not have a word that meant "ship." I had to use the words that meant "large canoe."

Tahni scrunched her eyebrows, then suddenly began speaking in a steady singsong voice, as if she was telling a very old tale of long ago and far away.

I scribbled as fast as I could.

"Hold on, hold on," I said, and held up my hand. She seemed to understand my request, for she began speaking more slowly. She pantomimed as she told the story. She was talking about her village, diving for pearls, fishing, playing. Then something happened—she was afraid, someone was chasing her. She was being taken captive.

She pointed to the picture of a Spanish galleon on the cover of one of the history books. *"Español,"* she hissed, and spat on the floor.

"Spaniards captured you? You were on a Spanish galleon?"

She nodded and her eyes glowed like burning embers.

"No, no, that's impossible. It must have been Cubans. Maybe it was a fishing vessel out of its territorial waters. Or maybe it was South Americans on an expensive yacht. Yeah, that's it—drug lords on a fancy sailing yacht."

Tahni's words came faster and her voice trembled. I barely had time to write everything down and knew it would take all night to decipher my writing. She was on a big ship, and so was her family. She was sad and crying—I'm not sure why, but it had something to do with her family.

Suddenly Tahni stopped in the middle of the story. Her eyes took on the familiar look of panic. The long black tress flew around her neck as she twirled around toward the porthole.

"Hurakan!" she whispered. *"Hurakan!"* She leaped up and ran to the porthole and pointed to the sky as she had done many times before.

I knew it was pointless, but I ran to the porthole, too. The sky was clear, with the setting sun shedding red beams on Jamaica's misty blue mountains.

"No, no, Tahni." I gently shook her shoulders. "There is no hurricane. No *hurakan.*" I shook my head. "No *hurakan.*"

Her dark eyes looked out toward the harbor, then back toward me, clouded over with confusion.

"Hurakan?" she asked softly.

I shook my head. "No."

Tahni was trembling all over and she felt even colder than usual, so I wrapped my arms around her and pulled her to the big trunk. She slumped onto it, then put her hands over her face and began to cry.

"Oh, no, not now," I groaned. "Tahni, come on, finish your story." I patted her shoulder and tried to comfort her, but she kept sobbing, *"Bogati, Bogati."*

Finally I got her to look up again. Her dark eyes glistened like wet obsidian and tears slid down her smooth cheeks. She sniffed and said some more words. I nodded and scribbled them in the notepad.

I heard my parents' voices out in the hall. I sighed.

"I have to leave now," I whispered, then quickly looked up the word for *good-bye.*

Tahni didn't protest—she just turned away and walked behind the overstuffed chair. I knew she would not come back out, so I sneaked out the door and got in step behind my parents, who were both dressed in Hawaiian shirts and shorts.

By the time passengers began loading into small wooden boats rocking in a narrow river, it was dusk. Trees with low-hanging vines obscured the sun, making it look even darker and spookier. All along the riverbanks, blazing tiki torches on bamboo poles lit the way, casting eerie yellow streaks across our faces. Fumes from the little motorboats gagged most of the passengers, but no one complained. A couple of naked kids bathed in the water and waved at us.

The luau wasn't exactly what I expected. There was no roasted pig, but there were a lot of barbecued meats and lots of fresh fruits and rum punch and tropical drinks with colorful little umbrellas stuck in them. It was eight o'clock, so I was starving.

The fire-eater was great. The audience groaned as he swallowed his flaming torches or spewed fire from his mouth. Up on the stage, women danced native dances, and a man who appeared to be made out of rubber inched his way under the limbo pole. Afterward a steel drum band played calypso and reggae music for the audience. Vanessa had been taking dance lessons every day aboard the ship, so she knew all the steps. My dad more or less stumbled along, mostly doing his version of the twist anytime the music got fast. Jessica danced with Brandon the hunk most of the time, and that left Jasmine for my partner.

The entertainment was okay, but all the while I thought about Friar Madrigal's little black book. Tahni had poured her heart out to me and told me her life story. His book lay in my room like the key to a newly discovered treasure chest. Without his little book, the notes in my pocket were useless.

We finally returned to the ship. My step-sisters were exhausted from bouncing around all night and fell asleep fast. Even the departing whistle screaming at ten o'clock that night didn't wake them up.

"At last," I whispered as I pulled out my notebook. With Friar Madrigal's list of vocabulary words and basics of grammar, I was able to piece together Tahni's story. I worked all night long, looking up words and trying to make sense of it all. I could not find many of the words, and some of the phrases didn't make sense. But I had read lots of books about the Arawaks and about the Spaniards, so I just filled in the gaps with what I thought would go best in Tahni's story. This is how it went, more or less:

"I am Tahni, and my village is called Bogati," her words began. I imagined her soft, sweet voice as I read the translation. *"I spent my days in happiness, weaving flower garlands, tending the* casavi *fields, helping my mother cook while my older brothers fished in the lagoon or*

wove hammocks to sleep in or while my father, the chief, prepared for festivals and batey games in the ball court.

"I loved everything about my village, but my favorite pastime was swimming in the sweet water of our lagoon and diving for pearls in the ocean. I love the water; it makes me feel calm and free as a dolphin.

"My village had no enemies, save for the evil Caribs, who sometimes attacked the other islands farther away. But our little island was far removed from the others and we had never been attacked during my lifetime.

"Then one day a strange, large canoe, with poles sticking up from its middle and puffed up cloth blowing in the wind, stopped outside the coral reef near our lagoon. Smaller canoes filled with strangers who had hair on their faces disembarked on our sandy beach. They called themselves Español."

"My father welcomed the strangers. We gave them food and water, and we girls placed flowers in their hair. At first the strangers behaved like friends. They gave us lovely round beads and tiny copper bells. We gave them cotton hammocks and seashell necklaces and pearls.

"But that night, while the village slept, the

strangers crept into our bohios and stole men and women and children from their beds. They tied our hands and loaded us onto the big canoes. They told us they were taking us to a big island where many Taino people lived and worked in large fields that grew strange plants.

"The sky was black with clouds that covered the moon and stars. My father warned the strangers that if they set out on the ocean that night, they would anger Hurakan, the mighty god of wind and rain. But the leader of the men laughed haughtily and ordered his crew to move the big canoe away.

"Once aboard the great canoe, the leader looked over all the prisoners. My blood turned cold when his evil eyes rested upon my face. He chose me to come with him to his sleeping place. He opened a door made of heavy wood and carved with vines and flowers and a beautiful shiny handle. Upon the handle was their sacred emblem, two sticks crossing each other.

"As the leader closed the door, my heart pounded with fear. The wind howled louder and the waves churned higher. Hurakan was angry that his children had been stolen. I tried to tell the stranger that Hurakan was angry, that he must turn the big canoe back around and return to the island to seek shelter. But the

Español *with greedy eyes spoke gibberish.*

"He chased me around the room. As his hands grabbed my hair, I felt fear as never before in my life. But at that moment, Hurakan screamed in fury and tossed the canoe high in the air. The stranger fell and hit his head. Blood trickled from his nose, and I knew that Hurakan had punished him for his evil ways. I tried to open the heavy door, but it would not budge.

"The winds howled louder, and the waves rocked the canoe until I could do nothing but sit on the floor and cling to the shiny handle. I cried for my father and mother and brothers. I heard the screams and cries of my people in the room next door, but they could not save me. I heard the cries of the terrified strangers as the canoe turned on its side and water rushed in through holes. I tried to get out through one of the holes, but it was too small. Water filled the room rapidly.

"As the water rose higher and higher, I lifted my face toward the sky and prayed to Hurakan to wash my body ashore to the sacred beaches of Bogati, my beloved island. Our people believe that if you die on Bogati, your soul joins those of your departed ancestors and

*your spirit lives happily forever. But if you die
in a strange place, or on the ocean, your spirit
must wander aimlessly, searching for Bogati.*

"*I am Tahni, daughter of the sea, and if I
can only find my precious island, my spirit will
rest in peace forever.*"

As I read the last words in my translation and
gently closed the notebook, there was no
doubt in my mind about one thing: the Spanish
galleon that had sunk with Tahni's family
aboard was the *Estrella Vespertina,* and the
brass handle on Cabin 102 was the very handle
that Tahni had so desperately clung to when
she died, almost five hundred years ago.

My heart ached with sadness as I pressed
my hand against the wall next to my bed. I
thought I felt Tahni's cool palm pressing
against my own.

"I swear I'll find your beloved island,
Tahni," I whispered. "And I'll set your spirit
free."

The Weather Report

I WOKE UP EARLY Saturday morning to find the *Historia* cruising through the Windward Passage, a narrow body of water between the two largest islands in the Caribbean. To the port side loomed Cuba, a mysterious dark green jewel. Off the starboard side, the mountains of Haiti glistened in the morning sun. *Haiti* was the Taino word for mountain. Mountains were sacred to them, for that is where they believed their race was born. As I watched the distant mountains, I remembered Lionel saying that the *Historia* used to stop at Haiti. But now there was a war and an embargo, so the liners just passed by the land of mountains.

My heart felt heavy and lonely all morning.

I missed Lionel and his stories. And besides that, he was the only person on this ship of fifteen hundred people who knew that something strange was going on in Cabin 102. If I told my parents that a charming Taino ghost lived in there, they would send me straight to the loony bin. They were on the verge of doing that anyway.

My cabin stewardess introduced me to the new chief steward of Calypso Deck, Preston, who was twenty-five years younger than Lionel. His plump rosy cheeks, very short blond hair, and short, stocky legs made him the complete opposite from Lionel. His precise accent and brisk, no-nonsense attitude were thoroughly British.

It was our family's turn to sit at the captain's table during lunch that day. Vanessa and her girls put on their finest sundresses, and even my dad slipped into a white Panama suit and tie. Man, he looked weird.

All the females at the table, from little Jasmine to a blue-haired retired piano teacher, gushed over the captain until I thought my stomach would turn. I suppose he wasn't bad looking; he had broad shoulders and good posture, and a great tan. But he was a lot older than my dad. The man had gray sideburns, for

Pete's sake. But that didn't seem to matter to the women at the table. They giggled and whispered and acted gaga when he stepped up in his snug-fitting, perfectly tailored white uniform. He bowed and snapped his heels after the maitre d' had introduced everyone at the table.

The food was even better than usual, tasty lobster in butter sauce and a dessert shaped like a chocolate rose with fresh raspberries around it. I'll say one thing for the voyage, I never ate so well in my life, and I know my dad and Vanessa never drank so many tropical drinks, either—Jasmine had a drawer full of the colorful miniature umbrellas.

The adults talked about a lot of silly, unimportant things—about the swimming pools, the casino tables, the upcoming grand finale show, and stuff like that. I was sitting very close to the captain, so I thought I would change the subject and ask something more interesting. I chewed my buttered croissant thoroughly, then cleared my throat.

"Excuse me, Captain. What exactly are the chances that this ship will get blown away by a hurricane in the next couple of days?"

The blue-haired piano teacher gasped and

my father stopped the slice of fresh pineapple that was on its way to his mouth. "Dusty!"

The captain chuckled. "That's a perfectly normal question, Dustin."

"Dusty, my name is Dusty."

"Of course. Even though hurricane season did officially begin two weeks ago, big storms rarely develop before August. I can tell you that during my fifteen years as captain of this ship, we have yet to encounter a hurricane during a June voyage. Now, September is another story altogether."

"But, just suppose there is a hurricane out there. Would you get a lot of warning beforehand? Would sirens go off or something like that?"

"There's no need for that, Dustin. We get advance notice in plenty of time to change course and steer clear of the storm. We have the most modern radar system available. And our radio crew is in constant contact with the National Weather Service in Miami. They know exactly where each storm is located and how fast it is traveling and how fast the winds are spinning. We don't just casually call in; we get hourly weather updates."

"But suppose your radios break down.

Suppose you can't contact the weathermen in Miami and a storm is coming."

"Dusty," my dad said in a whisper between clamped teeth, "don't be a nuisance."

The captain chuckled, but his pale blue eyes looked like he could kill me.

"If by some weird quirk of events this ship should get caught in a hurricane, I assure you that the *Historia* is able to withstand the mightiest storm. She has not survived for thirty years by coincidence. She is one of the best built ships afloat in the Caribbean."

"Yeah, but thirty years is so old," Jasmine said. Everyone at the table laughed at the cuteness, but I thought it was a very good observation.

The captain's face turned pink under that glorious tan, but he smiled a gleaming white smile.

"Why don't you come up to the bridge and visit the navigation room after lunch, Dustin? I'll be glad to show you the equipment and put your mind at ease. Tour the engine room, too, to see how strong the old girl is."

All right! At last I was going to get to see something interesting. I couldn't wait to finish lunch, but of course the adults kept talking and talking. I wondered if the captain didn't have anything better to do than gab, but finally he rose and showed me to the navigation room, next door to the pilothouse.

Radar equipment covered one end of the room, a jumble of knobs and computerlike consoles and tiny screens. A huge map of the world was spread across a table. A short, wiry man with bright red hair and a handlebar mustache leaned over it, taking measurements.

"Hello, Red," the captain said as he put his hands on my shoulders and steered me across the room. "Dustin here wants to know if there is a hurricane out there somewhere waiting to devour our good ship."

"That's Dusty," I corrected, and squirmed out from under the captain's hand.

Red straightened up and grinned a smile yellowed from years of smoking cigarettes.

"Aye, laddie, I've been tracking the storm all week."

My eyes flew open. "You mean there *is* a hurricane out there?"

"Well, not exactly a hurricane. She's just a colossal storm. But in the cold North Atlantic, she can do more than a wee bit o' damage. One oil tanker broke up and several oil rigs had to be evacuated near the Shetland Islands."

"Oh," I said with a sigh of relief. "Then that storm's not anywhere near us. It's nothing for us to worry about, right?"

"Aye, that's right. But my family lives in northern Scotland and I've got a brother on one of the derricks, so I'm keeping an eye on her."

"See, Dustin," the captain bragged. "There's no need to be concerned. Red and his crew watch every storm in the Western Hemisphere. They get plenty of warning." He pointed to a kind of fax machine that was spitting out longitude and latitude readings and weather reports. As a new one came in, Red marked the coordinates with a red pin on a map of the British Isles. I noticed that the nearest storm to the Caribbean was something off the coast of Africa, way across the Atlantic ocean.

"Are you satisfied now?" the captain asked. "Do you feel safer?"

I nodded. "Yeah, I guess so. Say, is that a map of the Caribbean islands?" I asked, pointing to sheets of paper that covered most of one entire wall.

"It's a navigational chart," Red said.

"Does it show every single island?"

"Aye. Every one. Even the tiny uninhabited ones. And it shows the water depths and the location of shoals and reefs and even old wreckages. We have to know where we're going, laddie."

"Where are the Bahama Islands?"

"Actually, the Bahamas aren't in the Caribbean," the captain said. "They're in the Atlantic, but a lot of cruise liners include them on the Caribbean cruises." He pointed to a group of islands south of Florida and east of Cuba.

"Are we stopping at any of the Bahama Islands?"

"No, but we'll be passing near them. There are over seven hundred islands in the Bahama chain. Some of the islands are fairly large, others are no more than specks of sand, tiny little uninhabited cays."

I studied the chart with hundreds of tiny islands peppered across the sea. How could I possibly figure out which island was the one Tahni called Bogati? Most of the smaller ones had no names and were uninhabited; a lot of them were privately owned by wealthy Americans and off limits. My only hope was that somehow Tahni would instinctively know which island had been her home. My dad had brought along his binoculars. With them I would be better able to see the islands.

When I arrived back at my room, I saw the new chief steward, Preston, standing in the hall right in front of our stateroom, talking to a cabin stewardess.

"Excuse me, sir," the stewardess was saying to Preston. "I need to talk to you about Cabin 102. Apparently someone has been sneaking inside. I found some clothing and an apple core. The apple appears to have been nibbled on by a mouse. I also saw some rodent droppings. I know Lionel was going to put out rat poison, but he never got around to it. Shall I do it now?"

My heart leaped to my throat and my brain scrambled into working gear.

"Uh, excuse me," I interrupted, squeezing my body between them. "I can explain all that stuff. Lionel let me go in Cabin 102 one day to get some old books to read. I was nibbling on an apple. I must have put it down on the dresser. I didn't see any mice."

"I see. And is this yours, too?" Preston held up Jessica's flowery blouse.

"So, that's where I left it." I slapped my forehead with my palm. "I was on my way to the laundry when I got distracted that day. My sister has been going crazy looking for that.

Sorry to disappoint you, but looks like there isn't someone sneaking in after all."

Preston tugged at his blond mustache and his blue eyes drilled a hole into mine. All of a sudden a scream pierced the air. I jerked open the door to my stateroom and saw Jessica standing in the middle of the room. Her face was dripping with water.

"That stupid faucet did it again!" she shrieked.

"Say, Preston, did Lionel also tell you about the faucet in my room?" I pushed the door open and pointed to the bathroom. "And the lights? They go off and on now and then. In my parent's room, too. I think you need to get a mechanic. I can tell you right now, Mom and Dad aren't very happy. They're talking about complaining to the captain."

"Oh dear. That won't do," Preston said. "We'll get on it right away."

Preston and the stewardess hurried down the hall. I could only hope and pray that they didn't mess around with Cabin 102 anymore.

"Thanks, Jessica," I said, patting her shoulder.

"What'd I do?"

"You may have just saved someone's life."

When I saw Jessica staring at her blouse, I tossed it at her.

"Is this yours? The steward found it in the hall a couple of days ago." I turned around fast, before she could say anything.

I desperately wanted to go inside Cabin 102 to check on Tahni, but Jasmine grabbed my hand and insisted I attend the children's award ceremonies. Jessica won an award for swimming in the mock Olympics and one for CPR. Jasmine won a prize for being friendly and one for helping others. Brandon won an award for weight lifting.

By the time the ceremonies were over, it was late afternoon. Nearly everyone I saw was preparing for that night's grand finale festivities. All the chairs in the beauty salons were full—women getting facials and manicures and hair treatments. Men wandered in and out of the barber shop, smelling like tangy aftershave lotion, and little kids took naps so they would be rested up.

All the heavy luggage had to be placed outside our doors in the hallway before midnight, so I changed into what I would wear that night and tomorrow and packed away everything else except for my pajamas. I helped Jasmine stuff her junk into her suitcase. She had to sit on it so I could lock the clasp. Jessica packed her clothes neatly and had no problems, except for the tons of souvenirs she had bought at the ports of call.

I returned all the books I had checked out of the ship's library, then curled up with a magazine in the reading area. But I couldn't concentrate on it. The ship was charging ahead at top speed of nineteen knots an hour. Around midnight the *Historia* would pass very near the Bahama Islands. Tahni's home, Bogati, was somewhere out there. It was one of those dots on the map, but which one? How could I get Tahni back home?

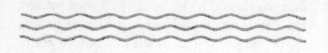

Hurakan Speaks

EVERY MAN, woman, and child had been hearing about the grand finale of the cruise since day one. The women dressed up in shimmery ball gowns or slinky cocktail dresses, bedecked from head to toe in jewelry. The men wore tuxedos or fancy suits and ties.

My dad tugged at his coat as we joined other passengers heading toward Lido Deck for the final buffet of the cruise. When we walked topside, we gasped in unison. Surely it was the most extravagant buffet ever created. I felt like I was at a Viking great hall feast and half expected to see Norse gods swoop down holding entire legs of lamb in their beefy hands.

The aroma of garlic and herbs and tomatoes drifted above tables that were lined end to end for what seemed like a hundred feet. Dish after dish of appetizing food covered crisp white linen tablecloths. Each platter of food looked like a piece of artwork, with vegetables shaped into flowers arranged into patterns. An elegant swan ice sculpture served as a centerpiece, and tropical flowers floated in a flowing pool of punch.

The tinkle of glass filled the air as waiters in white gloves bustled to and fro refilling champagne glasses. Laughter rose as the sun set over the western horizon.

After the feast, everyone retired to the showroom to watch the musical revue extravaganza. There was something for everyone—a very plump Elvis Presley impersonator in a white sequined suit, a country-and-western female vocalist in a red-white-and-blue sequined suit, and a Las Vegas–style floor show with dozens of women in feathers and skimpy costumes. Between all of the costumes, there must have been enough sequins to light up the sky.

All the while the dancers pranced and the singers crooned, I kept glancing at my wristwatch. The whole program was supposed to end around midnight. At that time everyone would go outside to Lido and Verandah decks to watch fireworks shot out over the ocean.

I had roughly calculated the distance we would travel and knew that we would be over the Great Bahama Bank about then, a stretch of shallow ocean. I had watched the crew dropping a notched rope with a lead weight overboard, sounding for depths at regular intervals. To the west was Cuba, to the east lay hundreds of tiny cays, making up part of the Bahama chain.

As the room echoed with applause at some antic on stage, I excused myself and slipped away. According to my calculations, we would probably pass within swimming distance of some of the smallest islands very soon. If I was going to bring Tahni to the upper deck and show her the islands, I had to do it now, before the floor show was over.

I trotted up to Verandah Deck. A sudden wind had come up, making the breeze even stronger than usual, forcing me to cling to the rail as I looked across the ocean. Even though the moon was shedding its silver light on the dark water, I could not see any islands. I saw some distant black specks, but that could have been anything.

I jogged down the stairs to Calypso Deck, stopping at my room long enough to grab my father's binoculars, a penlight, and Friar Madrigal's black book. I saw the pink conch shell on the dresser. I had not had a chance to give it back to Tahni since our last encounter. A twinge of guilt pinched my heart. I had made a solemn promise that I would help Tahni find her precious Bogati, yet I had not visited her for almost thirty hours. She probably thought that I had deserted her.

I checked the corridor to make sure no one was coming, then gently turned the brass handle on Cabin 102. It didn't budge.

"No!" I gasped. I rattled the door handle again and again, but it was useless. Preston must have locked it after the stewardess found the clothes.

I tapped lightly. "Tahni! Tahni, open the door," I whispered. But only silence came from inside the cold room. I knocked louder.

"Look, Tahni, I have your conch shell." I removed Father Madrigal's black book from my pants pocket and flipped through it until I found the Taino word for *conch*. But still Tahni did not reply.

A knot began to twist inside my stomach and desperation seized my heart as I bounded up the stairs two at a time. I strode to the deep swimming pool, the one that Tahni preferred. The buffet tables had been cleared away, the deck swept and mopped, deck chairs arranged in rows, and bottles of champagne nestled in buckets of ice in preparation for the fireworks. The entire deck was deserted now, and the unusually strong wind made me shiver.

I sat down beside the pool, then lifted the conch to my lips. I blew into it the way I had seen Tahni do. A low, mournful sound vibrated the air.

Where was Tahni? Had she given up on me ever coming to see her again? Did she know that the islands her people had once called Lucayan were growing near? Had she seen her beloved Bogati in the distance and jumped overboard without saying good-bye? I blew the conch again, as sadness swallowed my heart.

A giggle made me jerk my head up. I looked into the shimmering blue water and couldn't believe my eyes.

"Tahni!"

A glorious smile covered her face as she dove into the deep water, retrieved a shiny new quarter, then popped up beside me. She climbed out of the pool and gave it to me, then tugged at my hand.

"Dustee swim," she said in a playful, sweet voice. Even though I had on my best pants and shirt and wore my dad's binoculars around my neck, I threw my arms around her dripping body and hugged with all my might. She grabbed the conch shell and blew so loud, I was sure the whole ship would hear.

"Shh!" I said, but she ignored me. She dived in again and swam underwater, one hand holding the shell. She swam to the bottom, placed the shell there, then came back to me.

"Dustee swim, bring conch," she said, four Taino words that I now understood.

"No, Tahni, no," I said. "There is no time for games tonight. You have to swim home. Swim to Bogati."

"Bogati?" Tahni's eyes opened wide.

I fished Father Madrigal's little black book out of my shirt pocket and tried to find the right vocabulary words, shining the penlight on the pages.

"Tahni dive," she called out.

"No, Tahni, there isn't time." I glanced across the deck to make sure that none of the waiters had returned yet.

Tahni giggled as her slender legs climbed each step of the slide. When she reached the top, she poised for a swan dive. The sight of her was breathtaking as the silver moonlight flooded over her brown skin. She sailed through the air and dipped into the water with hardly a splash. She popped her head up on the other end of the pool and I let my breath out for the first time.

"Dustee dive," she shouted, and beckoned me toward the slide.

I shook my head and quickly moved closer to the snack bar, where the breeze wasn't so strong. Tahni followed me, still giggling and dripping water. I was flipping through the vocabulary, trying to find the words to say, *"Bogati is near, you must swim ashore,"* when I heard the grind of the elevator and the sound of people coming up the stairs.

"Shoot! The floor show must be over. Everyone's coming up here for the fireworks." My words had hardly come out of my mouth when a whine filled the air, followed by an explosion of gold and red off the port side.

Hordes of passengers flowed to the rails and *ooh*ed as they pointed to the sky. Soon another blast rocked the air, this time crackling silver and green.

I heaved a long sigh and grabbed Tahni's hand. I led her to the nearest lifeboat and we crawled inside and ducked down. I was sure no one would notice us in there. They would be too busy watching fireworks and drinking champagne. I searched through the vocabulary again until at last I had the words I needed.

"I've got it! *Bogati near, Tahni swim home,*" I said triumphantly in the Taino language, but when I looked up, Tahni was gone. I saw her stretching over the rail on the opposite side of the ship, away from the fireworks and the crowd.

"*Hurakan!*" she shrieked, pointing to the east. "*Hurakan!*"

"No, no, no!" I pounded my fists against the lifeboat, then leaped to my feet and ran to her side.

"*Shh,* Tahni, be quiet," I said, and desperately made hand motions at her. But Tahni was more hysterical than I had ever seen her before.

"*Hurakan!*" she screamed at the top of her voice.

I turned and looked in the direction she was pointing. The sky was clear, the moon was out, but there *was* something out on the ocean. Something about the horizon didn't look right.

I scrunched my eyes and stared but could not tell what it was.

"Maybe it's Bogati," I whispered hopefully as I lifted the binoculars to my eyes. At that moment a big ball of fireworks lit up the sky on the opposite side of the ship.

"That's not an island. Oh, man, it's moving—it's a mountain of water!"

I flew to the emergency box mounted on the side of the wall. Lionel had said that it had never been used in his thirty years aboard. *Well, there's a first time for everything,* I thought, as I flipped the red switch and a shrill, pulsating scream filled the air.

I ran down the metal steps from Verandah Deck to Lido Deck, where most of the passengers were gathered. They were looking up and around, still holding champagne glasses and laughing as if the emergency siren were part of the fireworks display. The captain, dressed in his finest white regalia, held a champagne glass in one hand and a walkie-talkie in the other.

"Find out who the devil pulled that switch," I heard him bark into the walkie-talkie.

As I passed the pool area, I jerked down one of the emergency life jackets and slid it over my shoulders. I tried to get people's attention, but they looked at me like I was an annoying ant at a picnic. In desperation I climbed up on top of a table and shouted:

"There are some giant waves coming! Go back inside or put on your life jackets!"

Suddenly I felt two hands grab me and yank me down.

"Russell! What's going on? Are you the one who flipped that switch?" My father shook me until I felt like my teeth were rattling. "Are you?"

"Dad, there're some big waves coming. One's at least fifty feet tall." I pointed to the east.

"That's impossible. The captain said there are no storms nearby."

"That doesn't matter, Dad. I read that waves can travel across the ocean for hundreds of miles. These waves might be from that storm in the North Atlantic or that one in Africa. When the swells go over shallow water, they get bigger and bigger. And we're near the Grand Bahama Bank right now. You have to believe me!"

My dad removed his glasses and squinted toward the east. But the dark swells on the horizon were too hard to see with the naked eye. I reached for the binoculars, only to discover that I had dropped them in my haste to get down the stairs.

"I don't see anything," my dad said at last, replacing his glasses. "Dusty, you've gone too far this time. When we get back you're going straight to a psychiatrist."

"You have to believe me!" I screamed, and jerked free from his grip.

The deck was covered with curious people, talking among themselves, speculating on what was wrong.

"Put on your life jackets!" I shouted to everyone I met. But by now the first mate had flipped off the siren, and the captain was speaking into his bright red bullhorn, reassuring people. When he saw me, his eyes spat fire.

"See here, Dustin. What's the meaning of this? This is totally irresponsible behavior. You've spoiled the whole fireworks program."

"Captain, I swear it's a giant wave. Look through your binoculars toward the east."

The captain scowled as he lifted his binoculars to his eyes, but when he saw the ocean, his lips parted in shock and his eyebrows shot up.

"Good Lord, man, look at the size of those swells. The biggest one looks to be over thirty

feet high. It'll be fifty by the time it reaches us."
He lifted a whistle to his lips and blasted out
an emergency sequence. He shouted into the
walkie-talkie.

"Flip the emergency switch, Ensign Leigh."
Seconds later the siren began pulsating again.
The captain lifted the bullhorn to his lips and
shouted:

"This is an emergency. Do not panic. Clear
the deck and return to your cabins. We are
about to experience some severe rocking. This
is not a drill. Clear the deck and return to your
cabins immediately. Do not panic."

The deck crew scrambled from below and
ushered people toward the stairs and the elevator. In spite of the captain's words, panic
flooded the deck. Women screamed, dropping
their champagne glasses. Men ran, stumbled,
pushed, and shoved to get to the doors.

I saw my dad herding Vanessa and Jasmine
toward the elevator, but it was packed, and so
was the stairway. At least twenty-five people
were still topside as the first large swells rocked
the ship. One man fell to his knees and crawled
to the elevator. Glasses toppled off tables
and lounge chairs scooted across the deck,
smashing against the rail or the snack bar, or

splashing into the pools. A new wave of screams filled the air as passengers struggled to keep their balance.

I grabbed a bar stool and held on tight as I looked to the east. This time I did not need binoculars to see the largest black wall of water approaching, growing larger as it moved across the shallow bank. Maybe it was just the wind I heard, but now it sounded like the evil whisper of a sea witch riding over the ocean toward us. At that moment I knew that not everyone would be able to get below before that giant wave hit us.

I grabbed a handful of life jackets from the swimming area and threw them to my dad. He tossed them to Vanessa and Jasmine, and to Jessica and Brandon, who were staggering down the stairs from the upper deck, gripping the handrail. Salty spray had already drenched Jessica's party dress.

My father and Brandon joined me, grabbing life jackets and hurling them to passengers who still waited their turn to get down the jammed stairs. When the last life jacket had been handed out, my father turned to me and his lips parted to speak.

That was when the granddaddy wave of them all hit the *Historia*. The deck tilted at a steep angle and salty black fingers smacked Lido Deck, sweeping it clear of people like a cleaning woman tossing a bucket of sudsy water over a floor.

Screams filled the air as passengers slid across the slippery wet deck toward the ocean. I felt my body flying through the air, then all I heard was the gurgling of water above as the ocean surrounded me, trying to squeeze the air from my lungs. Suddenly I realized that in my haste I had not tied my life jacket and it had slipped off when I hit the water.

I sank deeper and deeper. I tried to swim, but my legs would not move. Something was holding them, something was pulling me down. The old familiar panic raced through my body. I thought I heard a sea witch cackle: *You are mine now, you belong to me.* And I felt her icy hands wrap around my legs and pull me down, deeper, deeper into her watery cavern.

It got darker as I plunged deeper and my air supply slowly dwindled. So this was the end that I had always feared. All those nightmares about drowning were at last coming true.

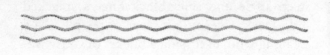

Freedom

I TRIED NOT TO THINK of sharks and electric eels and stingrays and poisonous jellyfish. I forced my brain to think of Tahni. From the moment I had seen the giant wave, I had lost track of her. I could only hope that she had heard my last translation and that she was now swimming toward her beloved island home. I imagined her swimming in the ocean as fast and sleek as a dolphin. If I had to die, at least it was a consolation to know that her spirit was free at last. And who knows, maybe we would meet again somewhere.

Suddenly Tahni was in front of me, laughing and doing somersaults and playing with the fish. She had a conch shell in one hand and a huge glimmering pearl in the other. A smile covered her face as she swam around me, like when a dog tears around the yard in wild, crazy circles when you first let it outside.

I wanted to open my mouth and call to her, but I dared not or water would have gushed in. I waved my arms in panic and she swam to me, a question in her dark eyes. Though we were underwater, she spoke in that sweet voice, and though she was speaking her own language, I understood.

"Why are you afraid, Dustee?" she asked. "You know you can swim as well as anyone. You have dived for the conch shell with me. You have nothing to fear. The ocean is not a wicked sea witch that wants to destroy you; the sea is a beautiful, loving mother that wants to take you in her arms and hold you like a child. Be calm, Dustee. Love her, and accept her love."

The words flowed into my head and heart and soon I felt my legs relaxing. The old feeling of paralysis faded away and I began to move them. Then I moved my arms. I was going up, up toward the surface. I saw a light above, a tiny silver orb. My lungs screamed in agony for air. I wanted to let go, to just open my mouth and let it all end swiftly, but I felt Tahni's hand on my shoulder. She guided me up toward the orb. Faster and faster I swam, until at last I thrust my head through the surface and saw the silver moon.

I gagged and coughed and sucked in air until my lungs were satisfied. I saw the *Historia* in the distance, a city of lights in a black sea. Her searchlights scanned the black water and her engines groaned as they slowed. But even if they had been switched to a full stop, it would take her thirty minutes to quit moving. I imagined the crew swiftly and expertly lowering a lifeboat, which would give them a much better chance of finding the passengers who'd been swept overboard.

I waved and shouted, but the ship was almost a mile away and still moving. No one heard me or saw me. No one but Tahni. She appeared beside me out of nowhere, and in her hand was my life jacket. I slipped it on and Tahni rested her hand on my shoulder. She did not mind being in the middle of the ocean in the darkness.

"*Bogati*," she said, her lips curved into a smile. She pointed toward a dark island in the distance. At least I thought it was an island. It was so small and so far away, I couldn't tell for sure.

"No, Tahni, I have to go in the other

direction," I told her. "I have to get back to the ship." I tried to swim toward the ship, but the *Historia* was still moving. Whether I liked it or not, the current was towing me in the opposite direction from the ship.

Tahni kept one hand on my shoulder all night long. We swam, then rested a few minutes, then swam again. Sometimes she grew impatient at my slowness. She would swim far ahead, turn and shout, and wave me on. But she always came back.

The moon traveled across the sky as the night wore on and morning approached. I was exhausted from fighting the wind and waves. I wanted to close my eyes and sleep forever, but Tahni kept prodding me and tickling me and singing songs and forcing me to stay awake. My arms felt as if they had been wrenched from their sockets and my legs felt like lead by the time the first tiny glimmer of pink dawn touched the eastern sky. The island was so close now that I could make out tiny palm trees swaying in the breeze and clean white beaches.

"*Bogati,*" Tahni whispered. Tears streamed down her face, and I knew she desperately wanted to leave me behind. But she held on to my shoulder and led me the rest of the way until I had passed over the coral reef and into a peaceful blue lagoon. I closed my eyes and let Tahni guide me to the white, powdery sands.

With a groan I staggered onto the beach and collapsed. The waves gently lapped at my feet, but I was too tired to move.

"I'm alive," I whispered. "I'm still alive." I breathed hard for a long time as my aching muscles rested. I was thinking of how wonderful some fresh, cold water would taste when I heard familiar laughter. I opened my eyes.

"Man," I whispered to the air. The lagoon was enshrouded in blue mist and the sinking moon was covered with a gray haze. Tahni was swimming and laughing as if the past few hours had been no more than a midnight swim to her. But she was not alone. I saw other boys and girls, some older, some younger than Tahni, swimming beside her. A young man popped up out of nowhere with a pearl as big as my thumb in his hand. Tahni clapped her hands in glee.

I heard adults cheering and saw men in long dugout canoes, spearing fish or casting out nets. Ashore, women laughed as they waved to Tahni. Some of them were cooking, others were stringing seashells into necklaces.

Babies and toddlers romped around their mothers. Three young women waded into the water and placed flowers around Tahni's neck and in her hair.

I saw a small canoe not far from me on the beach.

"Tahni!" I shouted as I grabbed the canoe and pulled myself up. She turned in my direction and waved. The other people did not even notice me, but Tahni swam to the edge of the lagoon.

"This is Bogati," she said. *"These are my people."* She pointed to the peaceful village with its palm-covered *bohios* surrounded by lush green plants and fragrant flowers and palm trees and colorful birds. *"I must leave now, Dustee. I must join my people. Thank you for being my friend, and for finding Bogati. Good-bye, Dustee."* She leaned closer and placed a soft kiss on my cheek. Even though she spoke in the Taino language, I understood every word she was saying. She swam several yards into the lagoon, then turned. A radiant smile beamed on her beautiful face as she shouted, *"Look, Dustee, I am free!"* She laughed and dived into the water like a dolphin.

"Good-bye, Tahni," I said. I tried to keep my eyes open, but the lids grew heavier and heavier as her laughter grew fainter and fainter. A deep, restful peace flowed over my body as I leaned my back against the little canoe and closed my eyes.

I woke up with the hot sun beating on my face.

"Over here!" someone shouted nearby. "Here's the missing boy!"

I rolled over and bumped into something hard, a tree trunk that had washed upon the beach a long time ago and was now weathered and spotted with barnacles.

"This was a canoe," I whispered to myself as I rubbed my eyes. In the brightness of daylight everything looked different. The lagoon twinkled like a sapphire. There was no mist. And now a quaint little hotel with coconut palms and little cabanas and a beach volleyball court snuggled along the shore where I had seen the Taino village.

I heard people shouting and the sound of feet running along the beach. Then I saw the waterlogged face of my father hovering over me. I almost didn't recognize him without his black-rimmed glasses.

"Are you okay, son?" he asked between

gasps to catch his breath. "You had one heck of a night."

I tried to climb to my feet, but instantly fell back down into a sitting position. My legs felt like rubber. I looked around and saw other passengers on the beach. Most of them huddled under blankets and sipped cups of steaming coffee.

"Is, is everyone all right?" I asked, scanning the beach. Suddenly I saw a streak of white-blond hair and tanned legs running toward me.

"Dusty!" Jasmine shrieked as her small legs sped over the sand.

She rushed to me and threw her skinny arms around my neck, chattering like a chipmunk, telling me about her adventure at sea. That voice that usually got on my nerves had never sounded so sweet. A few seconds later Vanessa was all over me, too, crying and kissing my cheeks.

"You saved our lives, Dusty," Vanessa said in a quivery voice. "Those waves came up so suddenly, if you hadn't warned the ship, a lot of people may have been killed. Because of you nearly everyone got below in time. The rest of us got into our life jackets just before the giant wave hit."

"Yeah, Dusty, you even saved the captain's life," Jasmine said cheerfully. "And Brandon's, too."

I glanced up at Jessica standing there in what used to be her fanciest party dress. Fat chance she would ever say thanks. She stared at me a minute, then sighed.

"Listen, kid, the next time you save my life, would you at least give me enough warning so I can change out of my best clothes? Look at this dress." She put her hands on her hips, then smiled and ran across the beach to where a bare-chested Brandon the hunk was wringing out his shirt.

"Come on," Dad said. "The cruise line is putting all of us up in that hotel tonight. We'll fly back to Miami by seaplane tomorrow morning. Let's get some rest and some food."

Early the next morning, while the rising sun turned the sand pink, we all walked down to the beach for a final look. The blond bunch slipped into rented snorkel equipment and splashed in the lagoon, while I sat on the beach soaking up the view. I could easily distinguish the line where the aquamarine sea turned darker blue, signifying deep water.

I heard a noise and saw Dad walking

toward me carrying an armful of snorkel gear. He dropped it at my feet.

"Well?" Dad asked, holding out a pair of flippers. "How about it, Dusty? One farewell dip in the blue lagoon before we leave?"

The old, familiar panic jumped all over me and the excuse machine kicked into working gear.

"After being in the water all night? Are you crazy?" The words started tumbling from my mouth. "Besides, I think I've still got some water in my lungs." *Cough, cough.*

Dad sighed and lowered the flippers. Defeat slumped his shoulders. "I was just hoping. But I guess I should know by now that you won't go swimming."

I saw the pain on Dad's face, and suddenly the excuses sounded stupid. I was tired, so tired of making them up. As he turned to go, I knew it was now or never. I could keep on lying to my father and have him hate me, or I could tell him the truth and have him think of me as a coward. I drew in a deep breath.

"Dad," I called out. "There's something I have to tell you."

"Yes?" He turned around.

"Dad, I know you love swimming. I mean, your old room at Grandma's house is lined with ribbons and trophies and stuff. And you wanted to be on the Olympic swim team."

Dad looked down at his bad knee and his hand rubbed it absentmindedly.

"That's true."

"And I know you're disappointed that I never took after you and joined the swim team—"

"Now, that's not true, Dusty. I never once tried to force you to join the team."

"No, but you were hoping I would. A blind man could see that."

Dad picked up a stick and twirled it in his hands a few seconds before answering.

"It was because you had so much potential, dern it. Because you were so good when you were a little kid. Why, you were swimming before you even learned to walk. I never saw anyone with so much talent. You could have broken every record I ever set, if you hadn't lost interest."

"I didn't lose interest," I said in a voice that sounded too small for my body.

Dad twirled the stick, then snapped it in two and tossed it aside. "Well, that's what it looked like to me. You lost interest. And nothing I did made you get it back." I saw

Dad's Adam's apple bob up and down as he swallowed hard. "Why, Dusty? Why?"

"Because—" The words stuck in my throat like a sharp bone. I swallowed again and again. My heart pumped faster and my fingers shook. I clenched my hands into fists and drew in a deep breath, deep enough to spew out seven years of pain and anger.

"Because I'm afraid of the water!" I shouted. "I've been afraid ever since I was five years old and almost drowned. And I didn't want you to know I was a coward. That's why!"

I turned and stumbled through the white sand toward the hotel, tears blurring everything around me.

"Dusty! Wait!" I heard Dad's voice behind me and the swish of his feet trotting over the sand. Suddenly his arms grabbed me and swung me around. He pulled me to his chest and squeezed so hard I couldn't breathe. Tears rolled down my cheeks, and no matter how hard I fought, I couldn't stop them.

"It's not your fault, son," he said, and kissed my head. "I should have seen it. I guess I was too busy with my own worries. If your mom and I hadn't been so busy fighting all the time, maybe we would have realized what was wrong. Shoot, if you'd fallen off a horse, we would have noticed right away."

"It's my fault, too," I said, sniffing and wiping my nose on my tee shirt. "I should have told you instead of keeping it a big secret."

Dad nodded and smiled. "You want to hear something funny? I had a big secret, too. I was terribly afraid of something just like you."

"You afraid? Of what?"

"I was afraid that you hated me. I thought you blamed me for the divorce. You never wanted to visit me at the beach house and you never wanted to swim with me in the ocean."

"Not because of you, because of the water."

He laughed lightly, then tousled my hair.

"See what happens when we try to keep secrets? No more secrets between us, ever. Is it a deal?"

"Deal! I'm through with secrets." I took his outstretched hand and shook.

"You know, considering how much you hate being in water, it was really brave of you to get through last night's ordeal. It's almost a miracle."

"Yeah, I guess you could call it a miracle."

"Does that mean you aren't afraid of water anymore?"

I shrugged. "I'm not sure, but there's only one way to find out. Let's swim."

"That's my boy!" Dad said.

We put on the snorkel gear and Dad walked with me to the edge of the lagoon. Slowly I waded out into the warm water, Dad not too far away.

"If you need me, son, I'll be here," Dad said, and gave me the thumbs-up signal.

When the water was chest high, I began to swim. At first I didn't let my dad get out of sight, then slowly I swam farther away. Soon the blueness of the water turned clear. I no longer felt those icy cold fingers pulling me down, but instead the water felt like warm brown fingers holding me up. I could see all the way to the bottom—seashells, oysters, rocks, sand, colorful parrot fish and clown fish, and beautiful butterfly fish coming and going, nibbling at my feet. I swam out farther and saw coral and seaweed and weird living things waving in the water. It was beautiful—oh, so beautiful.

My sisters and parents swam at their own pace, each looking and searching. Jasmine and Jessica swam over to me a few times, excitedly showing me some shell or trinket they had found. Vanessa and Dad waved at me occasionally.

I swam and swam, sometimes holding my breath and diving deep enough to pick up a shell or oyster from the ocean floor. One time down, I found a pink conch shell. It looked exactly like the one I had given to Tahni.

After a while we all splashed out of the water.

"How was your swim?" Dad asked anxiously.

"Beautiful, man," I chirped back. He grinned and tossed a hotel towel at me.

"It's almost time to call the taxi," Vanessa said, wrapping a towel around Jasmine's shoulders. "Time to say good-bye to paradise." She sighed.

"I'll be there in a minute," I said. "I just want to sit here a few more seconds." I removed my snorkeling gear and sat down in the cool, white sand.

As I stared across the turquoise water, I lifted the conch shell to my ear. Along with the sigh of the wind and the swish of the waves, I thought I heard Tahni's sweet voice whispering her last, fading words: *"Look, Dustee, I am free!"*

I drew in a deep, deep breath of sweet air tinged with the fragrance of flowers and the smell of the trees and salty air. I stood up and shouted to the ocean, "Look, Tahni, I am free, too!"

I brushed the sand from my legs, then ran across the beach to join my family.